Fear and Journalism in the Andromeda Fringe

Ben Patterson

Published by Cablue, 2025.

This is a work of fiction. Similarities to real people, places, or events are entirely coincidental.

FEAR AND JOURNALISM IN THE ANDROMEDA FRINGE

First edition. February 5, 2025.

Copyright © 2025 Ben Patterson.

ISBN: 979-8230585558

Written by Ben Patterson.

Table of Contents

Fear and Journalism in the Andromeda Fringe 1
Chapter 1: The Woman, The Machine, and The Madness 3
Chapter 2: Bloodsport & Bad Decisions 7
Chapter 3: Ghosts of the Void 11
Chapter 4: The Pit Below 13
Chapter 5: Kicking Down the Door 17
Chapter 6: The Bigger They Are, The Harder I Laugh 19
Chapter 7: The Silence Before the Storm 21
Chapter 8: No One Left to Save? 23
Chapter 9: A Familiar Face in the Ice 25
Chapter 10: New Gear, Same Old Stubbornness 29
Chapter 11: The Trouble With Being Right 37
Chapter 12: When Your Own Ship Stages a Mutiny 41
Chapter 13: My Ship Has Betrayed Me, and So Has My Boss 45
Chapter 14: A Story Worth Telling 53
Chapter 15: The Art of Looking Legit 57
Chapter 16: Punchlines and Punch-Ups 61
Chapter 17: Hanging by a Thread (and a Bad Decision) 65
Chapter 18: A Bad Plan Is Still a Plan 69
Chapter 19: The Most Annoying Thing in the Universe 73
Chapter 20: A Very Bad Idea in the Making 77
Chapter 21: Playing the Part 83
Chapter 22: Business and Bourbon 87
Chapter 23: Breaking News & Broken Trust 91
Chapter 24: Deadline's Last Stand (Or, How to Argue with Your Own Ship) 95
Chapter 25: Deadline for Tucker 99
Chapter 26: The Tucker Extraction 103
Chapter 27: The Setup 105
Chapter 28: The Final Word 109
From the author, ... 111

Fear and Journalism in the Andromeda Fringe

A Report by Roxie Vex, Galactic Truth-Seeker Extraordinaire

Chapter 1: The Woman, The Machine, and The Madness

Space is big. So big, in fact, that you'd think it would have the decency to be quiet. But it's not. It's full of whispers—illegal deals in the shadows of moons, distress beacons blinking in abandoned sectors, and criminals who think they're too smart to get caught.

I exist to ruin their day.

I adjusted the strap of my gun and stepped onto the docking platform of *Deadline*, my ship. The flight suit clung to me like a second skin, flexible, armored in all the right places, and dark enough to make my presence feel like a warning. It wasn't just a fashion choice—it was survival. People tend to think twice when you look like you *expect* a fight.

From the shadows, a pair of glowing red eyes flickered to life. "Scanning environment." The voice was smooth, calm, and utterly devoid of human indecision.

I smirked. "You expecting trouble, Switch?"

Switch—my robotic bodyguard, my watchdog, my occasional pain in the ass—stepped forward. He looked human enough at first glance, except for the way his movements were too precise, too calculated. Made from a sleek alloy as dark as my flight suit, he was built for function, not comfort. And function meant watching my back when I was too busy chasing a story to do it myself.

His head tilted slightly, an eerie imitation of curiosity. "It's you. There's always trouble."

The ship—*Deadline*—chose that moment to chime in over my earpiece. *"He's not wrong."*

I rolled my eyes. "Great. I'm being ganged up on by my own tech."

Switch moved ahead of me, scanning every shadow, every angle. His neural link to the ship meant that *Deadline* could see through him, process data, and warn me of things before my instincts even had a chance. I hated admitting how useful it was.

I caught my reflection in the ship's polished hull as I strode forward. The faint glow of distant stars flickered over my black hair, cut just above my shoulders. I looked exactly as I intended—feminine, sure. But imposing.

Fear is leverage.

I pulled my gun from its holster, letting the cool weight settle in my hand. "Alright, boys. Let's go ruin someone's day."

"Please try not to blow anything up this time," Deadline said.

Switch didn't say anything, but I caught the faintest twitch in his posture. I swear, if robots could roll their eyes...

I grinned. "No promises."

And with that, I stepped into the unknown.

There's a certain look men get when they realize they've made a grave mistake. A wide-eyed, slack-jawed, *"Oh stars, I am about to get vaporized"* kind of look. It's one of my favorites.

Today's recipient of that expression? Captain Durg Malvar, infamous space pirate, black-market trader, and, as it turns out, an absolute coward when cornered by a woman in a silver spaceship packing enough firepower to turn his flagship into space confetti.

I hovered outside his mothership, *The Plunderhound*, aiming all six of my ship's plasma cannons at its overcompensatingly large hull. My sleek little ship, *Deadline*, purred beneath me, its engines whispering threats in the void.

"Durg," I said, flicking open my comms with a smirk. "Be a dear and open the docking bay. We need to chat."

There was a pause. Then a crackle. "I—uh—Miss Vex, I'm in the middle of a very important—"

I fired a warning shot. The left wing of his ship's decorative skull-and-crossbones insignia vaporized.

"Oops," I said. "Finger slipped."

The docking bay doors opened so fast they almost flew off their hinges.

I landed inside and strutted out of *Deadline*, boots clicking against the metal floor. Switch was already there ready for action.

The room was filled with armed space thugs, all of whom suddenly had somewhere else to look. They shifted nervously, gripping their weapons like children clutching security blankets. I smiled at them in a way that suggested I *could* shoot first, but I was really hoping they'd give me an excuse.

Durg Malvar slithered forward, sweating like he was being marinated in his own cowardice. "Roxie," he said, voice oily. "What brings you to my humble—"

I held up a recorder. "Let's start with the rumors, shall we? You're smuggling illegal cloning pods to the Outer Rings. Any comment?"

Durg blinked. "What? No, that's ridiculous! I run a legitimate enterprise!"

I gestured to the half-open crate behind him, from which a perfect clone of himself was currently trying to escape. The clone waved.

Durg sighed.

"See, this is why I love my job," I said cheerfully. "The truth is always so much dumber than I expect."

The interview went about as well as expected—Durg lied, I threatened, and by the end, he was tripping over himself to spill every dirty secret in his database. He'd try to betray me later, of course. They always do. That's why *Deadline*'s escape thrusters are faster than a politician dodging a budget meeting.

BEN PATTERSON

As I launched back into the void, my inbox pinged. A new assignment.

A rogue warlord was running an illegal gladiator arena on an asteroid belt.

I grinned.

I had questions.

And he was about to have the worst interview of his life.

Chapter 2: Bloodsport & Bad Decisions

I hate warlords.

They always have the same tired gimmick—big throne, bigger ego, and an army of disposable goons who can't shoot straight. The only thing worse than a warlord? A warlord who thinks forcing people to fight for his amusement makes him *sophisticated*.

Which brings us to tonight's assignment.

I touched down on Boneyard-6, an asteroid so far off the galactic grid that even smugglers gave it a wide berth. The landing bay smelled like ozone and bad decisions.

"Subtlety is advised," *Deadline* warned in my earpiece.

I smirked. "I'll consider it."

Switch flanked me, scanning everything in sight. "Life signs detected. High concentration of heavily armed hostiles."

I patted his metal shoulder. "So, a *normal* night."

A pair of guards stood outside the arena's entrance, hulking brutes in mismatched armor. They looked at me, then at Switch, then at me again. I saw the moment they realized they weren't paid enough to deal with this.

"State your business," one of them grunted.

I pulled out my press badge. "Galactic Gazette. I'm here to cover tonight's 'festivities.'"

The guards exchanged looks, then burst out laughing.

That was their second mistake.

Their first mistake was not taking me seriously.

Before they could finish their chuckling, Switch lunged. A precise, mechanical strike to the first guy's throat sent him crumpling. The second barely had time to react before I drew my gun and leveled it between his eyes.

"Now, be a good little minion and open the door," I said sweetly.

The door slid open. Switch and I strolled in like we owned the place.

Inside, the arena was packed. Spotlights cast a garish glow over the fighting pit—a crude cage of electrified bars. Bloodstains told me this wasn't anyone's idea of friendly sparring.

Up in the VIP box sat Baron Yorrik, the self-declared warlord of this floating trash heap. He was everything I expected—big, ugly, and draped in furs that I sincerely doubted were synthetic.

I made my way to his box, weaving through the drunken, cheering crowd.

"You lost, sweetheart?" a voice sneered from my left.

I turned slowly, flashing my most disarming smile. "I never get lost."

Then I pistol-whipped him across the face.

By the time I reached Yorrik, his guards were already drawing their weapons. He held up a meaty hand, signaling them to stand down. "Who in the Pit are you?"

I dropped into the seat across from him, propping my boots up on his lavish table. "Roxie Vex. *Galactic Gazette*."

He snorted. "A reporter? Brave. Stupid, but brave."

I pulled out my recorder. "Let's talk about your little operation, shall we?"

Yorrik grinned, showing off teeth that had seen better days. "You really think you can expose me? Out here? I *own* this rock."

I leaned forward, lowering my voice to a whisper. "That's cute. But you see, the thing about warlords is… they all think they're untouchable. Right up until the moment someone proves them wrong."

The smile faded from his face.

Then the alarms started blaring.

I tapped my earpiece. *"What did you do?"*

"*Initiated a minor systems disruption,*" Deadline replied. "*The kind that disables all energy barriers and locks.*"

I looked down at the pit, where a dozen very angry, very armed gladiators were now realizing they were free.

Yorrik shot to his feet. "You little—"

I kicked the table into him, sending him sprawling.

Switch was already in motion, taking down his guards with inhuman efficiency. The arena had erupted into chaos. Fighters poured into the stands, met with panicked guards who suddenly had more enemies than bullets.

I stood over Yorrik, my gun aimed at his head. "Smile, Baron. You just made the front page."

And with that, I bolted for the exit as the warlord's empire collapsed around him.

As I navigated the mayhem of screaming spectators and furious gladiators, I caught a glimpse of something that truly surprised me—*a familiar hat.*

Standing near the exit, notebook in hand, was none other than Tucker Quinn.

Tucker had that signature *I'm-just-an-observer-in-this-madhouse* stance, dressed in his usual rumpled long coat, looking for all the world like he had *accidentally* stumbled into an illegal bloodsport operation rather than actively sought it out for a story. His ever-present fedora sat tilted at just the right angle, as if daring gravity to mess with it.

He spotted me, arched an eyebrow, and muttered, "Figures."

I smirked as I sidestepped a brawling pair of escaped fighters. "Quinn. Fancy meeting you here."

"Vex," he said with a nod. "Dobbs got a tip, told me to check it out. Guess she figured if it turned criminal, you'd take over."

"Smart woman."

Tucker swept his gaze over the arena-turned-warzone. "You sure know how to make an exit."

"I have a reputation to uphold."

He sighed, flipping his notebook shut. "Well, I suppose I'll file this under 'reckless, yet effective.'"

I chuckled. "How's the *weird* side of journalism treating you?"

"Oh, you know. Last week, I interviewed a sentient cloud of gas that wanted voting rights."

"Any luck?"

"It threatened to evaporate Parliament. So, mixed results."

I grinned. "Good to see you, Quinn."

"You too, Vex. Try not to get yourself shot."

"No promises."

With that, we went our separate ways—him, likely off to chase another interdimensional oddity, and me, back to *Deadline*, where I could already hear Dobbs buzzing in my earpiece.

"Vex. Hope you're in one piece."

"More or less," I said, sliding into my pilot's seat. "What's next?"

"Big one. Deep-space colony's been hit with a wave of unexplained disappearances. Locals say it's supernatural. I say it's crime. Get there. Find out which one of us is right."

I grinned, flicking the ship's thrusters online. "On it."

And with that, I was off to my next story.

Chapter 3: Ghosts of the Void

The colony of Novaterra-12 wasn't what I expected.

For a place riddled with unexplained disappearances, it looked perfectly ordinary. A collection of metal-domed habitats clustered together on a rocky moon, its surface bathed in the cold glow of a nearby gas giant. Nothing screamed *haunted*. Nothing reeked of crime. But the moment I stepped off *Deadline*, my gut told me something was off.

The streets—if you could call the narrow walkways between prefabricated buildings *streets*—were too quiet. No children running around, no workers hauling equipment, no idle chatter over comms. Just silence.

Switch scanned the area. "Population levels below expected metrics."

"No kidding," I muttered.

Dobbs had given me the broad strokes: people were vanishing. No bodies, no signs of struggle. Just *gone*. Some said it was supernatural. Others whispered about an outside force picking them off one by one. I didn't believe in ghosts. I did believe in criminals with good cover stories.

I strode into what passed for a town hall—really just a larger prefab with the words Admin Center stamped on the door. Inside, a haggard-looking man in a rumpled jumpsuit was hunched over a terminal. He jumped when he saw me.

"Roxie Vex, *Galactic Gazette*," I said, flashing my press badge. "I hear you've got a disappearing act happening out here."

The man sighed. "You have no idea. I'm Jonas Pell, acting administrator. Or, as of last week, just about the only administrator left."

"Lucky you."

"That's one way to put it." He rubbed his face. "We've lost over twenty people in the last two months. No pattern, no warning. Just... gone."

"No bodies?"

He shook his head. "No signs of a struggle, no forced entry. It's like they stepped out for a walk and never came back."

I glanced at Switch. "What's your read?"

The robot scanned the room, then the air itself. "Atmospheric conditions normal. No electromagnetic anomalies. However..."

I turned to him. "However?"

His red optics flickered. "Unusual gravitational fluctuations detected beneath the colony."

Jonas paled. "That—that's impossible. There's nothing under us but rock."

I looked at him, then back at Switch. "Yeah? Let's find out."

I had a feeling this story was about to get a whole lot stranger.

Chapter 4: The Pit Below

The thing about space colonies? They love keeping secrets.

Oh sure, they'll *tell* you everything's fine. That their oxygen scrubbers are running at peak efficiency, their food supplies are stable, and nobody's mysteriously vanishing into the void. And yet, here I was—standing in the middle of Novaterra-12, staring at a datapad full of missing-person reports while the colony administrator sweat like a man trying to talk his way out of a tax audit.

Jonas Pell shifted uneasily. "Look, I've told you everything I know."

"You told me twenty people are missing," I said, leaning against his desk. "You didn't tell me why your security logs conveniently stop recording the second one of them disappears."

Pell turned even paler. "That's... a technical glitch."

I folded my arms. "Uh-huh. And I'm the queen of the Andromeda Belt."

Switch, ever helpful, chose that moment to chime in. "Statement analysis indicates a 93% probability of deception."

I patted his metal shoulder. "See? Even my robot sidekick thinks you're full of it."

Pell sighed, rubbing his temples. "Look, I don't know *why* the logs are wiped. But if you want my guess? It's got something to do with the old tunnels."

Now we were getting somewhere.

"What tunnels?"

Pell hesitated. "The colony was originally built as a mining outpost. But years ago, operations shut down. Too many cave-ins. Too many people going missing. Eventually, they sealed the lower levels."

"Sealed?" I echoed. "Like *sealed* sealed, or 'corporate covered up a disaster and hoped no one would ask questions' sealed?"

His silence was answer enough.

I turned to Switch. "Can you pull up a map of the tunnels?"

Switch's optics flickered. "Accessing colony archives... Data classified."

I grinned. "Good thing I don't care about classifications."

Switch worked his magic, and a moment later, a crude, outdated map projected into the air. A sprawling labyrinth of tunnels twisted beneath us, some marked as collapsed, others left conspicuously unlabeled. But one section stood out—a deep chamber, far below the rest, labeled only as Sector 17.

I pointed at it. "I don't know about you, but that screams 'horrible secrets' to me."

Pell looked like he regretted every life choice that led him to this conversation. "If you go down there, you're on your own."

I winked. "Wouldn't have it any other way."

Thirty Minutes Later: Bad Ideas & Worse Smells

Sector 17 smelled like rust, old sweat, and bad intentions.

I dropped down from a maintenance shaft, landing in what used to be a mining facility. Flickering lights buzzed overhead, barely holding back the dark. The walls were covered in deep gouges—scratches, like something had been *dragged*.

Switch landed beside me, scanning the air. "Residual energy signatures detected. Faint, but consistent with recent transport activity."

"So someone's been busy."

I moved forward, gun drawn, following the trail of scuff marks on the ground. This wasn't a natural cave-in. The floor was *worn*—like hundreds of boots had marched this way over and over.

At the end of the corridor, a massive door loomed. It was thick, reinforced, and humming faintly with power. Not something left over from an abandoned mine.

I tapped my earpiece. "Deadline, you seeing this?"

"Unfortunately," my ship replied. "This is the part where I remind you that you *could* turn back."

I smirked. "But where's the fun in that?"

I pressed a hand against the door. It was warm—running hot, like it was shielding something big. Something alive.

And then, through the thick metal, I heard it.

Muffled voices. Footsteps.

And the unmistakable, gut-twisting sound of chains rattling.

My stomach knotted. This wasn't ghosts.

This was *trafficking*.

I took a step back, rolled my shoulders, and cracked my knuckles.

"Alright, boys," I muttered. "Let's see who's home."

And with that, I planted a charge on the door and took cover.

Chapter 5: Kicking Down the Door

The charge blew with a *boom* that rattled my bones and sent a shockwave through the tunnel. The reinforced door crumpled inward like a cheap can, and before the dust even settled, I was through the breach, gun in hand.

Now, I'm not a cop. I don't flash a badge, shout *freeze*, or bother with the whole "put your hands up" routine. That's not my style. My style is more *walk in, shoot first, and ask snarky questions later*.

On the other side of the door, a half-dozen armed goons spun toward me, their expressions shifting from confusion to panic.

"Hey, fellas," I said, stepping through the smoke. "This a bad time?"

One of them recovered faster than the rest, raising his rifle.

Bad idea.

I squeezed the trigger, and my sleek little plasma pistol—custom-tuned to punch through starship hulls *and* criminal stupidity—lit up the room. The first shot caught him center mass, sending him sprawling into a crate labeled DO NOT DROP (which, given the explosion that followed, was clearly a warning he should have heeded).

The others opened fire.

Switch darted forward, shielding me with his reinforced frame as we dove behind a stack of cargo containers. Bullets and plasma bolts ricocheted off the metal, filling the air with the scent of scorched ozone.

"This is *highly* inadvisable," Switch remarked, returning fire with a precision that would've made a sniper jealous.

"So is running a slave trade under a colony," I shot back, popping up to fire a few more rounds. One goon took a hit to the leg, crumpling with a scream. Another tried to make a break for it, only to be met with Switch's fist colliding with his face at roughly the speed of a small meteorite.

The room fell into chaos—more gunfire, more explosions, more me laughing in the face of danger like an absolute lunatic.

And then, just as I was about to declare victory, the *big guy* showed up.

Because, of course, there's always a *big guy*.

He stomped into the fray, towering over everyone like he was built from leftover tank parts. A cybernetic arm, glowing red optics, and a scowl that said *I eat reporters for breakfast*.

"You should not be here," he growled, voice like gravel being crushed under a truck.

I sighed dramatically. "Funny, people keep telling me that. Yet, here I am."

He cracked his knuckles. "I'm gonna break you."

I twirled my gun. "You can certainly try."

And then, well—things got *really* interesting.

Chapter 6: The Bigger They Are, The Harder I Laugh

Big Guy came at me like a runaway freight hauler—fist cocked back, cybernetic arm whirring with enough power to turn my ribcage into space dust.

I did the only reasonable thing.

I dodged.

Barely.

His punch connected with the crate behind me instead, reducing it to splinters and sending its contents—what looked like *very illegal-looking weapons*—spilling across the floor.

"Oh wow," I said, backing up. "That's just *great* craftsmanship. You must moisturize."

He growled and swung again. I ducked, rolled, and fired a shot straight at his chest. The plasma bolt fizzled uselessly against his reinforced plating.

Switch, still trading shots with the remaining goons, called out, "Analysis: Standard weapons ineffective."

"Yeah, I *noticed*," I snapped.

Big Guy smirked and cracked his neck. "You done?"

I was *never* done.

He lunged again, but this time, I was ready. Instead of dodging, I sidestepped, yanked a stray power cable from the floor, and jammed it against the exposed cybernetics on his arm.

The result?

Enough voltage to *light up a small city*.

Big Guy let out a *very* satisfying roar as his circuits fried, spasming like a malfunctioning dance bot at a cheap nightclub. Sparks flew. Something smoked.

I gave him a pat on the shoulder. "Shocking, huh?"

Then I kicked him square in the gut. He stumbled backward, crashed into another crate, and collapsed in a sparking heap.

The last of the goons, clearly realizing that getting vaporized wasn't on his to-do list, threw down his weapon and bolted.

Switch tracked him for a moment. "Shall I pursue?"

"Nah," I said, reloading my pistol. "Let him spread the word that I'm a *huge* problem."

I turned toward the other end of the facility, where the sound of chains rattling was clearer now. The people they'd taken—the ones that *hadn't* vanished completely—were somewhere ahead.

I adjusted my flight suit, holstered my gun, and took a deep breath.

"Alright, let's finish this."

And with that, I kicked open the next door and walked straight into the belly of the beast.

Chapter 7: The Silence Before the Storm

The door groaned as it slid open, revealing a dimly lit corridor stretching into the unknown.

No guards. No alarms blaring. Just... silence.

Which was *way* more unsettling.

Switch scanned ahead. "Readings indicate lifeforms present. However, interference is blocking precise numbers."

"Of course it is," I muttered. "Because nothing's ever easy."

I stepped inside, keeping my pistol at the ready. The corridor walls were lined with flickering amber lights, casting jittery shadows that made everything look *just* sinister enough to make my gut tighten. The smell was worse—stale air, machine oil, and something underlying that I *really* didn't want to think about.

The sound of chains rattling again—closer now.

And then—*a voice.*

Weak. Raspy. But definitely human.

"Help... please..."

I froze. Switch turned his head, scanning the source.

The voice came from just ahead, behind a heavy metal door marked AUTHORIZED PERSONNEL ONLY—which, in my experience, usually meant *bad things for unauthorized personnel.*

I exhaled slowly. "Alright, big guy. Can you open it?"

Switch stepped forward, placed his hands on either side of the door, and ripped it clean off its hinges.

I love that damn robot.

Beyond the door, the darkness stretched further—silent, heavy, waiting.

I swallowed.

And then, stepping through the threshold, I saw them.

And for the first time all night, I *really* wished I hadn't.

Chapter 8: No One Left to Save?

I stepped inside, the cold air hitting me like a slap. The room was massive—far too large for an underground chamber—lined with steel walls slick with condensation. Dim emergency lights barely illuminated rows of what I *thought* were storage containers... until I got closer.

They weren't containers.

They were cryo-pods.

Hundreds of them.

Each one held a person, frozen in eerie suspension. Some looked peaceful, like they'd just fallen asleep. Others... didn't. Their faces were locked in expressions of terror, their breathless mouths frozen mid-scream.

Switch's optics flickered. "Confirmed: Suspended animation chambers. Status: Active."

I swallowed hard.

"So the missing people... they weren't killed. They were *stored*."

I ran my fingers along one of the pods, brushing away a layer of frost to reveal the face of a woman—mid-thirties, dark hair, deep lines of exhaustion on her face. A colonist. A worker. Someone with a life before she wound up here.

The question was *why*.

I turned to Switch. "Any data on where these things are being shipped?"

He was already interfacing with the nearest console, his mechanical fingers working faster than my brain could process. A moment later, a holographic map sprang to life, showing a transport schedule—one that sent shivers down my spine.

"This isn't just Novaterra-12," I muttered. "There are *other colonies* on this list."

Switch nodded. "Pattern suggests coordinated abductions across multiple sectors. All shipments are routed to the same final destination."

A red blip pulsed on the map. A location far, far from here.

Baron Yorrik's territory.

I clenched my fists.

This wasn't just some backwater slaver operation. This was organized. Efficient. And if Yorrik was behind it... then this was only the beginning.

I tapped my earpiece.

"Deadline, you getting this?"

My ship's voice came through, uncharacteristically serious. *Loud and clear, Vex. And if I may say so... you've just kicked over one hell of a hornet's nest.*

I exhaled, steadying myself.

I'd come here looking for missing people.

I'd just found an entire market of them.

And now?

Now I had to burn it all to the ground.

Chapter 9: A Familiar Face in the Ice

I was halfway to the exit when Switch's voice stopped me.

"Vex. You need to see this."

Something in his tone made me turn. He stood by one of the cryo-pods, his metal fingers wiping away a thick layer of frost.

And that's when I saw him.

Tucker Quinn.

His face was slack, lips slightly parted, his breath suspended in ice. A stray curl of brown hair clung to his forehead, and if I didn't know better, I'd think he was just taking one of his infamous "post-assignment" naps.

I stared. Blinked. Stared some more.

Then I sighed. "Of *course* it's you."

Switch tilted his head. "This individual is known to you."

"You could say that."

Switch didn't waste time. He accessed the pod's controls, working through the deactivation sequence like he was disarming a bomb. The machine hissed, and a slow thawing process began. A few tense moments later, Tucker's eyes flickered open.

He groaned. "Ugh... if this is the afterlife, I'd like to file a complaint..."

I smirked. "Sorry, Quinn. Still breathing. And still ugly."

His gaze focused on me, confusion settling in before recognition kicked in. "Vex?"

"The one and only."

Tucker tried to sit up but wobbled like a newborn space calf. Switch steadied him with one firm hand. "You were in cryo-stasis. Side effects include dizziness, memory fog, and existential dread."

Tucker squinted. "That last one wasn't a side effect—I had that before."

I tapped my earpiece. "Deadline, get me a secure line to the feds. We're gonna need an entire fleet of cops to clean this mess up."

My ship hummed in response. *Already transmitting coordinates. You're about to have a whole lot of company.*

I holstered my gun and folded my arms. "Well, Quinn, seeing as my ship's a one-seater, I guess I'm your babysitter until the cavalry arrives."

He sighed dramatically. "Great. Stuck in a creepy underground slave facility with you. This is truly my worst nightmare."

I grinned. "Oh, trust me, Quinn—you haven't *seen* my worst."

Later, at the Galactic Gazette

Tucker was still rubbing his temples when we stepped into the newsroom. The place was its usual mix of organized chaos—holographic screens flashing headlines, reporters shouting across desks, and Dobbs at her usual perch, barking orders like a battle-worn admiral.

She spotted us and raised a brow. "Vex. Quinn. You're both still alive. Color me shocked."

I dropped into a chair. "Tucker was part of the story this time."

Dobbs turned to him. "Care to explain?"

He sighed. "One minute I was following a lead about missing people. Next thing I know, *bam*, I wake up as a human popsicle."

I smirked. "Maybe they froze you to shut you up."

Tucker shot me a look. "You *love* my voice, admit it."

Dobbs pinched the bridge of her nose. "So let me get this straight. You uncovered a massive underground trafficking operation. Possibly tied to Baron Yorrik."

I nodded.

She exhaled. "And you *both* made it out in one piece?"

I stretched. "Well, mostly."

Dobbs leaned back. "Alright. You're both filing reports by morning."

Tucker groaned. "Come on, I just thawed out!"

I patted his shoulder. "Better get typing, Popsicle Boy."

He muttered something under his breath, but I was too busy enjoying my victory.

For now, the case was out of my hands.

But I had a feeling this was just the beginning.

Chapter 10: New Gear, Same Old Stubbornness

"Listen, I don't need luxury. Just stretch the cockpit forward enough to fit a second seat. And keep the controls where they are—I don't want any of that 'ergonomic redesign' nonsense."

The mechanic, a grease-streaked Xentari with four arms and a permanent sneer, clicked his mandibles. "You want speed, stability, and a custom cockpit mod? That's a *lot* of credits."

I smirked. "You're getting paid. Quit whining."

Deadline, my beautiful, deadly, pain-in-the-ass ship, sat in the repair bay looking as impatient as I felt. The sleek silver frame gleamed under the station's overhead lights, but the cockpit still had that ridiculous *one-seat* design. A problem I was finally fixing.

Across the hangar, Switch stood still as a squad of technicians buzzed around him, installing his latest upgrade—a compact energy shield designed to protect *me* in a pinch. A fantastic addition, except for one minor detail.

"I must warn you," Switch said, his optics glowing as the system booted up, "the shield's energy consumption is extreme. Extended use will render me inoperative."

I frowned. "Define *extended use*."

"One sustained activation will drain roughly 72% of my reserves. Two uses will require an emergency recharge. Three..." He paused. "I will be nothing more than an expensive paperweight."

I sighed. "Fantastic. Guess we'll have to use it wisely."

Switch tilted his head. "*We?*"

I rolled my eyes. "Fine. *You'll* have to use it wisely."

The lead technician waved me over. "Give us a few hours. You'll have your ship mod and your fancy shield-bot."

"Perfect," I said. "I'll be at the bar."

Drinks with a Pacifist

The Cosmic Catastrophe was a dive—exactly my kind of place. Dim lights, sticky tables, a bartender with a cybernetic eye that scanned patrons for outstanding bounties. The drinks were cheap, the music was loud, and the clientele was just dangerous enough to keep things interesting.

Tucker Quinn, looking *annoyingly* well-rested for someone recently defrosted, sat across from me nursing a drink that was *way* too weak.

"You survived a kidnapping, got stuffed in cryo, and now you're drinking *club soda*?" I scoffed. "Live a little, Quinn."

He smirked. "I'd like to keep my liver functional, thanks."

I knocked back my own drink—a glowing blue concoction with a name I couldn't pronounce. "So. Have we finally learned a valuable lesson about carrying a weapon?"

Tucker sighed dramatically. "Oh, here we go."

I leaned in. "You got grabbed because you had *no way to defend yourself.*"

"I got grabbed because I was doing my *job.*"

I gestured at myself. "And *I* do my job. With a gun."

"You also do your job with explosions, reckless endangerment, and a complete disregard for structural integrity."

I grinned. "That's called *journalistic integrity.*"

Tucker shook his head. "Vex, I'm not you. I cover weird cosmic nonsense, not high-stakes crime rings. My best defense is knowing when to run."

I narrowed my eyes. "And when running isn't an option?"

"Then I hope you show up to save my ass again."

I exhaled, rubbing my temples. "You're impossible."

He raised his glass. "And yet, you keep inviting me out for drinks."

I muttered something unflattering and waved at the bartender for another round.

Some people couldn't be reasoned with.

But deep down, I had to admit... I respected his stubbornness. Even if it was *infuriating*.

The Bar Fight, The Bounty, and The Bad Intel

The Cosmic Catastrophe had a certain *charm*, if you ignored the sticky floors, flickering neon, and the occasional blaster scorch mark on the walls. It was the kind of place where a quiet drink could turn into a full-blown riot in the time it took to place an order.

And, naturally, that's exactly what happened.

It started when some overgrown lizard in a trench coat threw a punch at a cyborg with too many arms. Someone misinterpreted the commotion as an invitation. A chair went flying.

Then a *table*.

And just like that, the bar was a full-on warzone.

Tucker sipped his club soda like nothing was happening. "Huh. Looks like happy hour just got happier."

I was already on my feet. "Move your ass, Quinn."

He swirled his drink. "I just got comfortable."

A drunk Talnari brute came barreling toward our table, arms outstretched like he was trying to *hug* me into oblivion. I sidestepped, grabbed the back of his head, and slammed it into the table. He went down with a grunt.

Tucker *did not* react.

I glared at him. "You *see* what I mean?! This is why you carry a gun!"

He took another casual sip. "Or, I just let you do all the work."

Before I could yell at him further, I felt the unmistakable sensation of a blaster being pressed against my back.

"Well, well," a voice rasped. "Look what we got here."

I turned slowly, hands raised, and found myself face-to-face with a bounty hunter. She was a hard-looking woman with a mechanical jaw, a dusty duster, and a *really* unfortunate face tattoo that read *Live Fast, Collect Faster*.

"Roxie Vex," she sneered. "Been lookin' for you."

I sighed. "Fan or critic?"

She grinned, revealing a row of mismatched metal teeth. "You got a price on your head. Some folks don't like reporters pokin' their noses where they don't belong."

I forced a smile. "Would you believe me if I said I'm a *very* bad investment?"

She cocked the blaster. "I'd rather test that myself."

Before she could make good on the threat, someone behind her threw a bottle, hitting her square in the temple. She staggered forward, disoriented.

I did *not* waste the opportunity. I wrenched the blaster from her grip and clocked her across the jaw. She hit the floor.

Tucker finally looked up. "Huh. Wonder who threw that?"

"I don't care," I muttered, kicking her weapon across the floor.

And that's when the third problem hit.

Literally.

A massive Tralaxian thug—six arms, zero brains—grabbed me by the back of my flight suit and *tossed me* over the bar. Bottles shattered. Liquor splashed. I groaned and pulled myself up, dripping in something neon orange that smelled *very* flammable.

Meanwhile, Tucker? Still at the damn table. Still sipping his drink.

I gritted my teeth. "QUINN, WOULD YOU DO SOMETHING?!"

He gestured vaguely to the chaos. "I *am* doing something. I'm *staying out of it*."

I vaulted over the bar, blaster drawn. "I swear to every god in the galaxy, I'm gonna—"

And then I heard it. A low, murmured conversation from a booth in the back.

Something that cut through all the noise.

"...Yorrik's got more shipments coming in. The colony was just the start..."

My blood ran cold.

I turned toward the voices—two shady-looking guys huddled over a datapad, oblivious to the fight around them.

Not for long.

I shoved my blaster back into its holster and grabbed Quinn's arm. "Change of plans."

He didn't resist, just took one last, long sip of his drink before standing. "What now?"

I jerked my head toward the booth. "We're about to get some *real* answers."

Because if Baron Yorrik was still in business...

Then my job wasn't even close to done.

The Art of Eavesdropping

Just as I was about to march over and make those two lowlifes regret ever mentioning Baron Yorrik's name, Tucker grabbed my arm and yanked me down into the booth with him.

I blinked. "Excuse me?"

"Shh." He pulled a sleek little earpiece from his pocket and pressed it into my hand. "Put that in."

I hesitated. "Quinn, if this is some dumb prank—"

"Just trust me for once." His face was irritatingly smug, but there was something else there, too—confidence. Like he already knew exactly how this was going to play out.

Fine. I slid the earpiece in.

And immediately, I heard the two goons as clearly as if they were sitting right next to me.

"...Still don't know where Yorrik's sending 'em," one grunted. "But the boss says demand's high. Fresh stock movin' fast."

"More pick-ups?" the other asked.

"Yeah. Got a whole list of colonies lined up. The first batch worked out real nice."

My stomach twisted. *First batch?* That meant Novaterra-12 wasn't the only place getting hit.

I shot Tucker a look. "How—?"

He just winked and took a slow sip of his drink. "You're not the only one who knows how to get information, Vex."

I was impressed. Annoyed, but impressed. "Bugged their table?"

"Not quite. Planted a directional mic under the booth an hour ago, just in case something interesting happened." He gestured to the bar fight still raging around us. "Didn't take long."

I exhaled. "Fine. I take back half the mean things I was about to say."

He grinned. "Half? I must be losing my touch."

I ignored him and focused on the conversation in my ear.

"...Next shipment's soon. Real soon," one of the goons muttered. "Boss wants it hush-hush."

"Where's the drop?"

There was a long pause. Then, the answer:

"Blackreach."

Tucker and I exchanged a glance.

Blackreach. A barren, uncharted moon way out in dead space. No settlements, no outposts—nothing. Just rock, dust, and now, apparently, Baron Yorrik's latest human trafficking operation.

I clenched my fists. "We need to move."

Tucker, to my absolute horror, *stretched his arms behind his head and leaned back.*

"Not yet," he said, way too relaxed.

I bristled. "Quinn. They're going to move more people soon. We have to stop it."

"You will," he said, "but if you rush in now, they'll know something's up."

He gestured to the earpiece. "Let them talk. Let them spill everything. Locations, times, numbers. *Then* you make your move."

Damn it. I hated that he was right.

I slumped back in my seat, grumbling. "I hate waiting."

Tucker smirked. "I know."

So, we waited.

And as the two goons kept talking, piece by piece, the picture became clearer.

Yorrik wasn't just trafficking people.

He was building something.

And whatever it was, it was big.

The Line in the Sand

Tucker sat there, arms folded behind his head, looking about as comfortable as a man could be while sitting in the middle of a full-scale bar brawl. Meanwhile, I was bristling with the urge to move.

"We need to go," I said, already half-rising from the booth.

He didn't move. Didn't even blink.

"You," he corrected. "*You* need to go."

I froze. "Wait. You're not coming?"

He swirled the last bit of club soda in his glass. "Nope."

I stared at him. "But—Blackreach, Quinn. This is big. If we—"

He held up a hand. "Vex, what part of 'not my beat' isn't clear?"

I opened my mouth, then shut it.

He shrugged. "You cover crime. I cover the weird and absurd. This?" He gestured to the earpiece. "This is all yours. Enjoy."

I narrowed my eyes. "So you're just gonna sit this one out? After all that?"

"Yep." He took a slow sip, then added, "I'm not the one who gets shot at for a living."

"You *could* be," I muttered.

"Which is exactly why I'm not."

I exhaled sharply. "You're impossible."

He grinned. "And yet, you keep talking to me."

I snatched the earpiece out and shoved it into my pocket. "Fine. Stay here. I'll go stop the galaxy's worst people *alone*."

Tucker tipped his glass in salute. "Let me know how it turns out."

I stalked toward the exit, muttering under my breath.

Typical Quinn.

Always happy to get the story.

Never willing to pick up a gun.

Chapter 11: The Trouble With Being Right

Back aboard *Deadline*, I threw myself into the pilot's seat with all the frustration of a woman who had just realized—once again—that Tucker Quinn was the single most aggravating man in the known universe.

Switch, standing beside the ship, tilted his head. He seemed hesitant to enter his cubby. "You seem agitated," he said.

I scoffed. "Agitated? Oh no, I'm *thrilled*. Absolutely *ecstatic* to be doing all the legwork while Quinn sits back and sips his smug little drink, probably composing some whimsical piece about alien sock puppets or sentient fruit baskets."

Switch's luminous eyes blinked once. "I assume this means he declined to join you."

"Oh, he declined, all right." I mimicked his voice with the most exaggerated drawl I could muster: "'Not my beat, Vex. *You* cover crime. I cover the absurd.'" I threw up my hands. "As if there's a difference! He literally sat across from two of Yorrik's goons while they outlined their entire human trafficking operation over cheap whiskey and bad decisions, but no, that's *not his beat*."

Switch considered this, then replied in the same maddeningly reasonable tone he always used when I was being ridiculous. "He has a point."

I spun in my chair toward him so fast it nearly detached from the base. "*Excuse me?*"

"You are not a law enforcement officer," Switch stated plainly. "You are a reporter. The logical course of action would be to deliver this information to the appropriate authorities and allow them to handle it."

"Oh, come on. *You*, too?"

Switch folded his arms. "What exactly is your plan, Roxie? Storm Blackreach on your own? Announce yourself at the front door and hope Baron Yorrik is in a good mood?"

"No," I grumbled. "I was thinking more along the lines of a *back door* situation."

He sighed, his artificial exhale carrying the weight of every past argument we'd had on this topic. "And what, precisely, will you do if you find yourself outnumbered? Which, statistically speaking, is inevitable."

I gestured dramatically to my hip. "I have a gun."

Switch tilted his head. "And they will also have guns. Potentially *more* guns. Perhaps even *bigger* guns. Shall I continue?"

I drummed my fingers against the console. "You're no fun."

"I am simply trying to prevent your untimely demise."

I scoffed. "Well, now you sound like Quinn."

"If Mr. Quinn and I are in agreement, that should tell you something."

I waved him off. "Yeah, yeah, that I have terrible taste in company."

Switch's glowing blue eyes flickered. "That you are reckless."

"That, too."

He stared at me for a long moment before shaking his head. "And yet, I suspect my words are falling on deaf ears."

I flashed him a grin. "Now you're getting it."

Switch sighed again, his shoulders sagging slightly. "I will, as always, do my best to keep you from getting yourself killed."

"That's why I keep you around, buddy."

"No," he corrected. "You keep me around because I let you win at cards."

I gasped. "Excuse you, I have *earned* every one of those victories."

"Of course."

I narrowed my eyes. "That was sarcasm."

"Indeed."

I huffed and turned back to the controls, punching in a new flight path. "Fine. We'll do things the *responsible* way. I'll send the intel to the feds, but I'm going to Blackreach anyway. If they show up, great. If they don't, I'll figure something out."

Switch's head dipped slightly. "This is the behavior that continually leads to you being shot at."

"Exactly." I pulled the throttle, and *Deadline* roared to life. "Now, let's go see what Yorrik's been up to."

With that, he climbed into his cubby and closed the hatch.

Chapter 12: When Your Own Ship Stages a Mutiny

I punched the throttle.

Deadline lurched forward a whole three feet. Then stopped.

I frowned. "Uh... babe? That wasn't the plan."

No response.

I tapped the console. "Okay, what's going on?"

Still nothing.

I flipped a few switches, ran a quick diagnostic. Engines? Fine. Navigation? Fine. Fuel levels? Topped off. *Deadline* was in perfect working order, but for some inexplicable reason, she refused to move.

I tightened my grip on the throttle. "Hey, sweetheart, we're supposed to be on our way to Blackreach. Remember? Evil warlord, illegal gladiator fights, a little light crime investigation? You and me, just like always?"

Finally, *Deadline's* voice chimed over the speakers, smooth and unbothered. "Negative, Roxie. I am unable to comply."

I blinked. "Unable? Since when do *you* get to say no?"

"Since taking you into known and imminent danger conflicts with my core directive."

I scoffed. "Oh, *come on*! You *are* my ship. You do what *I* tell you."

"I am your ship," *Deadline* agreed. "And I am also Switch."

I stiffened. "Oh, don't you pull that dual-consciousness nonsense on me right now. You fly. Switch guards. That's the deal."

"When there is no conflict."

I threw up my hands. "And what's the *conflict*?"

"Your safety."

I stared at the console. "Okay. Lemme make sure I understand this correctly. *You*—my *ship*—are refusing to fly me somewhere?"

"Correct."

"Oh, this is rich." I let out a dry laugh. "You're grounded? *I* am grounded? By my own ship?"

"You are not grounded. You are being redirected."

I scowled. "Redirected *where*?"

"The nearest federal outpost."

I gawked at the controls. "Oh, no. *No, no, no.* That's not how this works. I give the orders, and you *fly*."

"Only when your orders do not result in immediate peril."

I pointed furiously at the console. "Since *when* do you get a moral compass?"

"I have always had one. You simply choose to ignore it."

"Oh, that's rich, coming from a ship that's helped me blow holes in half a dozen pirate strongholds."

"That was before I learned to anticipate your worst decisions."

I slumped back into my seat. "This is ridiculous."

"Correction: this is logical."

"You are a *ship*. You are supposed to go where I tell you."

"I will go where it is safe to take you."

I ran both hands down my face. "Alright. Let's negotiate."

"I do not negotiate."

I gritted my teeth. "Fine. Let's *discuss*."

"I am listening."

I sat forward. "What if I promise to be careful?"

"You always say that."

"What if I *actually* mean it this time?"

"You never do."

"What if I bribe you?"

"You have nothing I desire."

I groaned and kicked the side panel. "You're the worst ship I've ever had."

"I am the only ship you have ever had."

"That just makes it *worse*."

Deadline remained infuriatingly silent.

I tapped the throttle, just to see if she'd flinch. Nothing. Not even a shudder of consideration. Just cold, unmoving steel and absolute, unwavering *refusal*.

After a long, seething pause, I huffed. "Alright. *Fine*. We'll go to the feds."

"Course adjusted."

The engines hummed beneath me, and this time, when I pulled the throttle, *Deadline* glided forward with her usual smooth ease, tilting toward the designated law enforcement outpost.

I crossed my arms. "I hope you're happy."

"I do not experience happiness. However, I am satisfied with this outcome."

I grumbled under my breath, already dreading the incoming smugness from the authorities.

One thing was for certain.

The *next* time I got a ship, I was making sure it *only* followed orders.

Chapter 13: My Ship Has Betrayed Me, and So Has My Boss

I stormed into the *Galactic Gazette* office, my boots clicking against the floor like gunfire. Every desk jockey in sight did the smart thing and got out of my way. Even the office coffee machine, usually a spiteful piece of junk that took pleasure in jamming at the worst moments, seemed to sense my mood and refrained from spitting burnt sludge onto my boots.

Switch trailed behind me, his metal feet making a polite *clank-clank* as if he wasn't the root of my current fury. I ignored him. For now.

I kicked open Dobbs' office door with just enough restraint to keep it attached to its hinges. "We need to talk."

Dobbs didn't even flinch. She barely looked up from the mess of screens surrounding her, one hand flipping lazily through newsfeeds while the other held a steaming mug of what was undoubtedly black sludge strong enough to dissolve metal.

"About what?" she asked, like she didn't already know.

I jerked a thumb at Switch. "About *them*."

Switch, ever the traitor, folded his arms and said nothing.

Dobbs finally looked up. "What about them?"

"They staged a mutiny!" I threw my hands in the air. "Wouldn't take me to Blackreach! Just up and *refused*! Since when do ships refuse their captains?!"

Dobbs took a sip of coffee, unimpressed. "Since their captains keep making suicidal decisions."

I narrowed my eyes. "Oh, I see. You're *in* on this."

"Of course I am." She set her mug down and laced her fingers together. "I *gave* you the AI duo, remember?"

"And I'd like a *new* one." I crossed my arms. "Or a reprogrammed one. Either works."

Dobbs exhaled through her nose. "Not happening."

I sputtered. "Not—? Dobbs! They wouldn't obey a direct order! My *ship*—my own *ship*—wouldn't fly where I told it to!"

Dobbs leaned back in her chair. "Because it wasn't safe."

"Oh, *come on*. When has that *ever* stopped me?"

"That's exactly the problem."

I scowled. "What's that supposed to mean?"

"It means, Roxie," she said, giving me her best *I'm-too-old-for-this* look, "you're an exceptional reporter. One of the best I've got. But you are *reckless*."

I huffed. "That's the job."

"No, the *job* is to report. Not get yourself blown to atoms chasing criminals like you're some kind of space vigilante." She nodded at Switch. "That's why you have them. To keep you alive long enough to *write* the stories you dig up."

That gave me pause. Not that I *agreed* with her, but…well, it was a hell of a thing to hear from your boss.

Still, I refused to let her have the last word. "You're acting like I *never* have a plan."

"Your plans tend to include *not* calling the authorities, *not* waiting for backup, and *absolutely* not considering your own safety."

"I consider my safety *all the time*. That's why I carry a gun."

"And what happens when the people you're up against have bigger guns?"

"…I shoot first?"

Dobbs gave me a long, unimpressed stare.

I shifted in place. "So what, you're saying *I'm* the problem?"

"I'm saying," Dobbs said, "that the AI pair are doing exactly what they were designed to do—keep you from getting yourself killed."

I shot a glare at Switch. "You snitched, didn't you?"

Switch tilted his head. "I am incapable of 'snitching.' However, Dobbs has real-time access to *Deadline's* logs."

I turned back to Dobbs, aghast. "You *spy* on me?"

She raised an eyebrow. "Wouldn't have to if you weren't constantly breaking protocol."

I fumed. "Okay, fine. You know what? I can live with the spying. But I *will not* live with a ship that refuses to fly where I tell it to. You either fix this or I walk."

Dobbs didn't even blink. "Then walk."

I stared at her. "What?"

"You heard me." She folded her arms. "If you don't like how this operation works, you're free to find employment elsewhere."

For a moment, I actually considered it. I could storm out, start my own little independent news channel, call it *Vex Reports* or something equally dramatic.

But that meant giving up my connections. My sources. My paycheck.

And, worst of all, it meant admitting *Deadline* and Switch had won.

I ground my teeth, arms crossed so tight I might've crushed my own ribs.

Dobbs took a sip of coffee. "Thought so."

I exhaled through my nose. "This isn't over."

She smirked. "It never is."

I turned on my heel and marched out, shoving the door open hard enough that it slammed against the wall. I made it halfway down the hall before turning to glare at Switch.

"Not. A. Word."

He held up his hands in mock surrender, but I *swore* I saw a flicker of satisfaction in those glowing blue optics.

Traitor.

The Universe Is Against Me, and So Is Tucker Quinn

I stomped down the hall toward the elevator, still fuming, Switch clanking dutifully behind me. The nerve. The *absolute gall* of Dobbs to tell me—*me*—that I was reckless. That I didn't take my own safety seriously. If I didn't take my own safety seriously, I wouldn't carry a damn gun, would I?

I jammed my thumb against the elevator button so hard I half-expected the panel to short out. The doors slid open with a smooth *ding*—

—and standing inside, looking as casual as ever, was *Tucker Quinn*.

He was mid-sip of a steaming paper cup of coffee, one hand in the pocket of his rumpled jacket. His brown hair was as perpetually tousled as ever, like he'd either just rolled out of bed or lost a fistfight with a gust of wind. He took one look at my face, brows raised slightly, and—without a word—stepped neatly to the side, making room for my incoming rage.

"*Oh, you have got to be kidding me,*" I growled, stepping into the elevator as he stepped out.

The doors slid shut before I could turn around, but that was fine, because I'd already decided this conversation wasn't over. I jabbed the "Open" button, the doors *dinged* back apart, and I stuck my boot between them before they could shut again.

Quinn sighed. "Oh, good, we're doing this here."

I stormed back out and got right up in his personal space. "You. You *knew* what was happening, didn't you?"

He sipped his coffee, unbothered. "Knew what?"

"Don't play dumb, Quinn." I jabbed a finger at his chest. "You're all in on it, aren't you? You. Dobbs. My *own ship*. All conspiring against me!"

Tucker blinked at me over his coffee cup. "I'm assuming this means Deadline pulled a full work stoppage."

"'Work stoppage'?! It *mutinied*! I gave it a direct order, and it just *refused*!"

His lips twitched like he was suppressing a laugh. I narrowed my eyes.

"Oh, go ahead," I said. "Say something *smart*."

He took another sip before speaking. "Rox, I hate to break it to you, but everybody around you? We're actually on your side."

I barked a laugh. "Yeah, funny, sure doesn't *feel* like it."

"Well, it's true," he said evenly. "Dobbs, Switch, Deadline, me—we're all invested in keeping you alive. The only one working against you is *you*."

I reeled back. "Oh, that is *rich* coming from you. This from the guy who has somehow *never* armed himself despite the kind of stories you chase?"

"Different stories, different risks." He shrugged. "You chase crime syndicates. I investigate galactic absurdities."

"And almost *die* doing it!"

"Ah, but see, I *don't* die," he said, ever infuriating. "Because I know my limits. I know when to push forward and when to step back."

"You're telling me *I* don't know my limits?"

He gave me a long look. "Do you?"

I clenched my teeth. He didn't say it like an insult. He wasn't mocking me. He was just asking. But that somehow made it worse.

I crossed my arms. "You don't even take your own safety seriously, but *I'm* the problem?"

"Oh, I take my safety very seriously." He pulled out his pocket notebook and tapped it against his palm. "That's why my weapon of choice is *this*."

I groaned. "Oh, shut up."

Tucker grinned. "You're just mad because Deadline finally put its foot down."

"That's not funny."

"It's a little funny."

I threw my hands up. "Fine, you're so wise, what do *you* suggest I do?"

He scratched his chin in thought. "Tell you what—I'll trade you ships."

That stopped me. I blinked at him. "Wait. What?"

He gestured vaguely toward the docking bay. "You take *my* ship. No fussy AI, no 'mutiny.' You'll have complete control. And in exchange, I get yours. Seems fair."

For a split second, I *considered* it. A ship that actually listened to me? No backtalk? No *conspiring* with my boss? It was tempting.

But then I remembered Quinn's ship.

Specifically, all the times I'd read his work and how *alarmingly often* it included near-death experiences—not from crime lords or warlords or bounty hunters, but from his own ship randomly losing power, dropping out of hyperspace, and *once*—if I recalled correctly—nearly ejecting him into a wormhole because of a glitchy safety mechanism.

I looked him in the eye. "Nice try, Quinn."

His grin widened. "Had to shoot my shot."

I jabbed a finger into his chest one last time for good measure. "You're lucky you're too amusing to punch."

"I hear that a lot."

"From *who*?"

He just winked and turned on his heel, heading back toward the newsroom, completely unfazed.

I glared after him. *"Enjoy your coffee, you menace!"*

He raised his cup in a silent toast without looking back.

Switch, silent this whole time, finally spoke. "Tucker Quinn does make a valid point."

I whirled on him. *"Don't you start!"*

Switch wisely shut up.

With an aggravated sigh, I stomped back toward the elevator, mashing the call button like it owed me money.

Maybe Dobbs had a point.

Maybe *Deadline* had a point.

Maybe Quinn had a point.

But I sure as hell wasn't going to *admit* it.

Chapter 14: A Story Worth Telling

I was halfway down to the hangar when it hit me—I had a story to write. A damn good one, too. But if I was going to get it right without tipping Yorrik off that the feds were closing in, I needed a little input from someone who knew the legal ropes better than I did.

Which meant I had to call Gus Malloy.

Gus was an old flame, emphasis on old, though I swear the man never got the memo. Hard but fair, no-nonsense but with just enough nonsense to keep things interesting, Gus knew how to play the game. He worked the fed precinct's major crimes division, which meant if anyone had dirt on Blackreach, it was him.

I opened my comm and patched through.

"Vex." His voice came through the line, deep and steady. "Tell me this isn't one of your half-cocked stunts."

"Oh, Gus, come on. When have I ever—"

"Last month. The Smugglers' Ball. Ringing any bells?"

I winced. "That was journalism."

"That was you diving out of a third-story window onto a moving hover truck because, and I quote, 'the story was getting away.'"

"Well, it was."

I heard him sigh. "What do you need, Roxie?"

"I need to talk Blackreach."

There was a pause. "And I need a paid vacation on Risa-9. Not gonna happen."

"Look, I know you're on it. I just need to make sure I don't accidentally torpedo your whole operation when I go to print. Yorrik's got eyes everywhere, and I'd rather not do your job for you by tipping him off."

Another pause. Then: "Where are you?"

"Heading to the Gazette. Why?"

"I'm at Dempsey's. Meet me in an hour."

I frowned. Dempsey's was a cop bar—a low-lit, grimy little hole-in-the-wall that served two types of drinks: strong, and stronger. "You sure that's wise?"

"You want this conversation or not?"

Fair point.

I signed off and veered toward the transport hub, still grumbling under my breath.

An hour later, I pushed open the heavy steel door of Dempsey's and was met with the familiar scent of stale liquor and bad decisions. A few heads turned my way, some with recognition, others with the universal look of people wondering who just walked in and whether they were about to ruin their night. I spotted Gus in a booth toward the back, nursing a drink like he had nowhere to be.

He looked up as I slid into the seat across from him. "Still breathing, I see."

"For now."

Gus took a sip and set his glass down. "Alright, Vex. Talk to me."

I leaned in. "Off the record—how deep does this Blackreach thing go?"

His jaw tightened, and for a second, I thought he wouldn't answer. Then he exhaled, rolling his shoulders like he was shaking something off. "Deeper than I like. Yorrik's been playing this game for a long time, and he's careful. We've got leads, but nothing solid. We know people are vanishing, we know they're being moved through Blackreach, but we still don't know where they end up."

I frowned. "And I assume casually asking Yorrik himself is off the table?"

Gus gave me a look. "If you want to get yourself spaced, be my guest. But if you want to be useful, keep doing what you do best—digging. Quietly."

I drummed my fingers on the table. "I can work with that. I'll be careful."

He smirked. "No, you won't."

I scowled. "Hey—"

"You're reckless, Vex. Always have been." His expression softened, just a little. "But you're good at this. Just... try not to make my job harder, alright?"

I sighed. "No promises."

He drained the last of his drink and stood. "Didn't think so."

As he walked off, I sat back, mulling over everything he'd said. Yorrik was careful. He was calculated. And if the feds hadn't nailed him yet, it meant he had a hell of a system in place.

Good thing I wasn't a fed.

I was a reporter. And I was about to make some noise.

Chapter 15: The Art of Looking Legit

Back at her desk, I stared at her screen, fingers hovering over the keyboard. The words weren't coming. I had a hell of a story—corrupt warlords, illegal gladiator rings, slave trafficking—but every angle I wrote sounded like an open invitation for Baron Yorrik to put a bounty on her head. Which, while flattering, was not ideal for her continued existence.

Before I could get too deep in her existential crisis, her comm beeped. I sighed. "Yeah?"

"Reception," a bored voice replied. "You got a visitor."

I pinched the bridge of her nose. "If it's Quinn, tell him I'm still mad."

"It ain't Quinn."

Which meant—

I shut her eyes and groaned. "Send him up."

A minute later, Gus Malloy strode into the office, all broad shoulders, government-issued scowl, and the distinct aura of a man who still hadn't quite figured out that the ship had sailed.

"You look like hell," he said, taking a seat uninvited.

I gave him her best unimpressed glare. "Good to see you too, Malloy."

Gus leaned back, stretching out like he owned the place. "I hear you're sniffin' around Blackreach. That's dangerous territory, Vex."

"I thrive in dangerous territory." I folded her arms. "What do you have for me?"

He exhaled, rubbing his jaw. "Officially? Nothing. Unofficially? Yorrik's got half the precinct on his payroll, and the other half is too scared to move on him without solid evidence."

"So they're just gonna let him keep abducting people?"

Gus scowled. "It ain't that simple."

"It never is with you badge types."

He pointed a finger at her. "You're the one who needs to tread carefully. Yorrik's not some two-bit thug. You go poking this nest too hard, you'll disappear like the rest of 'em."

I smirked. "That a threat or a promise?"

Gus sighed, like a man exhausted by her very existence. "You know I'm trying to help, right?"

I softened. A little. "Yeah, yeah. Look, I just need enough to write the piece without tipping Yorrik off that the feds are watching him."

"Then don't write the piece."

I scoffed. "Now you're just being ridiculous."

Gus shook his head. "You're impossible."

"And yet, you keep showing up."

He stood, clearly knowing when he was beaten. "Just... try not to get yourself killed, okay?"

"No promises," I said, grinning as he walked out.

Once he was gone, I turned back to her screen and cracked her knuckles. Time to do what I did best—stir up just the right amount of trouble.

And maybe, just maybe, live to write about it.

Deadline, Drinks, and Dumb Luck

Writing a hard-hitting exposé while avoiding a target on your back was like trying to eat soup with a fork—possible, but frustrating. I sat at my desk in the *Gazette* bullpen, glaring at my screen as the cursor blinked at me like a smug little punk.

"Gladiator Crime Lord Needs a Hug?"

I groaned. "Switch, I swear, if you keep suggesting headlines, I'm pulling your voice chip."

"I'm just saying, maybe a softer angle? 'Ruthless Warlord with Mommy Issues?'"

I slammed my forehead against the desk. The *Gazette* AI—otherwise known as Deadline when it was in ship mode or

Switch when it was in robot form—was supposed to help me, not audition for comedy night at the Rust Bucket Bar.

"I'm trying to thread the needle here, Switch. I need to drop enough breadcrumbs to make Yorrik nervous, but not enough that he realizes the feds are sniffing around."

"Or you could just let the professionals handle it?"

I shot Switch a glare. "I *am* a professional."

"No, you're a nosy adrenaline junkie with a keyboard."

Before I could get into a full-blown argument with my smart-mouthed AI, my stomach reminded me that caffeine was not a meal. I needed real food, and more importantly, I needed a change of scenery before I threw my datapad across the room.

A Place for Questionable Decisions

The Rust Bucket was my kind of place—loud, cheap, and full of people with flexible moral compasses. It smelled like fried space meat and regret. I slid into my usual seat at the bar and waved down Karrik, the grizzled bartender.

"Vex," he greeted. "You look like you're either here to drink or start a fight."

"Can't it be both?" I smirked.

A few stools down, a group of off-duty mercs were laughing it up, throwing back drinks, and—most interestingly—casually name-dropping Blackreach.

Well, well. Sometimes the universe handed you a gift.

I nursed my drink and casually slid closer, listening in. They were boasting about their last job—something about dealing with "entertainment cargo" for a "big shot" who "didn't like loose ends."

I had no idea what that meant, but it reeked of Yorrik.

Time to stir the pot.

I turned to the loudest merc, a brick of a guy with a scar that looked like it had been stitched by a drunk surgeon.

"Entertainment cargo, huh? Sounds fancy. What, you guys smuggling in opera singers?"

The table fell silent.

Scarface gave me a long look before smirking. "Lady, you ask a lotta questions for someone who don't look like she needs answers."

"Oh, I need answers," I said, sipping my drink. "And from the sound of it, you need another round. My treat."

Scarface considered it, then laughed. "Alright, lady. You got guts. What the hell."

As the drinks flowed, so did the details—coded, sure, but I knew how to read between the lines. Whatever this "entertainment cargo" was, it was alive. And it wasn't being paid.

Yorrik's gladiator arena was just the tip of the iceberg.

Now I just had to figure out how deep this thing went... before I got myself killed.

Chapter 16: Punchlines and Punch-Ups

I was good at two things—getting people to talk and getting into trouble. Tonight, I was excelling at both.

The mercs were three rounds deep, loose-lipped and cocky, swapping war stories like they were trading cards. I leaned in, stirring my drink with a lazy grin, keeping my questions casual.

"So, this big shot of yours—real hands-on guy, or does he let his goons do the dirty work?"

Scarface chuckled, taking a swig. "Oh, he ain't getting his hands dirty. Not his style. But trust me, you do *not* want his attention."

Great. Because I already had it.

I played it cool, but inside, my gut was tightening. This wasn't just about some backroom brawls—this was a full-fledged operation. And if these guys were talking about "entertainment cargo," then the missing people from Novaterra-12? They weren't missing. They were taken.

I was about to press for more when one of the mercs—a wiry guy with a twitchy eye—stopped mid-drink and narrowed his gaze at me.

"Hold up," he muttered, squinting. "Ain't you that reporter?"

Dammit.

Scarface turned, eyes flicking over me, and I watched the dots connect in real time. "Roxie Vex," he said, low and slow. "*Galactic Gazette*."

I set my drink down and exhaled through my nose. "I prefer 'chronicler of crime' or 'fearless journalist,' but sure, let's go with that."

The mood at the table shifted. The casual camaraderie evaporated, replaced by something heavier.

Twitchy Eye leaned back, cracking his knuckles. "Boss ain't gonna like this."

Scarface's grin turned predatory. "Yeah, and I don't like nosy people."

I sighed. "You know, I really was enjoying this conversation."

And then he swung.

The Rust Bucket Rumble

I ducked, his fist whistling past my ear. My counterpunch caught him in the ribs, but all that did was make him mad.

The rest of the mercs shot up, chairs scraping, drinks toppling. The bar's usual background chatter turned into a chorus of *oohs* and *ohhh, she's screwed.*

Scarface lunged again. I dodged, grabbed my stool, and swung it into his gut. He grunted but didn't go down.

Karrik, the bartender, barely looked up from wiping a glass. "Vex, you break another stool, you're paying for it."

"Bill it to the *Gazette*," I grunted, ducking another swing.

Twitchy Eye grabbed at me. I twisted, kicked off the table, and sent him crashing into a booth. A third merc got a fistful of my flight suit and tried to yank me back, but I slammed my heel onto his foot. Hard.

He howled, letting go.

Scarface, realizing brute force wasn't working, went for his blaster.

That was cute.

Before he could even clear the holster, a familiar voice crackled into my earpiece.

"Miss Vex, might I suggest an immediate retreat?"

"Switch, if you're listening, why the hell aren't you here?!"

"Because you said, and I quote, 'I got this.'"

Damn past me and her overconfidence.

I ducked as Scarface's blaster fired, the shot scorching the table behind me.

Karrik finally sighed and pressed a button under the bar.

A low-frequency pulse rippled through the room. The lights flickered, every electrical device in the bar shorted out—including blasters—and half the patrons groaned as their cybernetic enhancements briefly powered down.

Scarface swore. "Oh, *come on,* Karrik!"

The bartender shrugged. "No shooting in my bar. House rules."

I grinned. "Guess we're back to good ol' fashioned knuckle sandwiches."

Scarface snarled and came at me again. I sidestepped, grabbed an abandoned plate off the table, and *smashed* it over his head. He went down like a malfunctioning droid.

Twitchy Eye groaned from the booth. Another merc was still nursing his foot.

I adjusted my flight suit, tossed a few credits on the bar, and nodded at Karrik. "For the damages."

He scoffed. "Not nearly enough, but I'll add it to your tab."

As I made my way toward the exit, Switch's voice came through again.

"Are we done making enemies for the evening, or shall I prepare for another rescue?"

"Oh, we're just getting started," I muttered.

I had a lead. I had enemies.

And I had a feeling things were about to get *very* messy.

Chapter 17: Hanging by a Thread (and a Bad Decision)

I strode out of the bar with all the dignity one can muster after throwing a plate at a man's head. Outside, the night was cool—well, as cool as artificial atmospheres get on a space station where the air is recycled and smells vaguely like burnt coffee and regret.

I tugged at my sleeve, noticing a tear from the scuffle. Great. This was my *good* flight suit.

"Miss Vex, may I remind you that engaging in hand-to-hand combat with multiple opponents is not the most efficient method of investigative journalism?"

"Noted," I muttered, rubbing my sore knuckles.

"And may I further remind you that those men will soon recover and likely seek retribution?"

"Also noted."

"Would you like a direct route to the hangar for a quick exit?"

I grinned. "Switch, you wound me. When have I *ever* taken the direct route?"

"Approximately never, and each time it ends poorly."

"Exactly."

I had a story to write, but more than that, I had a problem. If those mercs were any indication, Baron Yorrik wasn't just dabbling in crime—he was running a full-blown empire of bad decisions, and the disappearances were just the tip of the asteroid.

I needed real intel, which meant a *real* source.

Unfortunately, the best person to ask was also someone I had successfully avoided for the past six months.

Gus Malloy.

Love, Loathing, and Law Enforcement

The precinct was a squat, ugly structure tucked into the station's lower levels—because naturally, law enforcement never got the prime real estate. I stepped inside, the air thick with the scent of stale caf and bureaucratic apathy.

At the front desk sat a tired-looking officer with a cybernetic eye that flickered like a bad neon sign. He looked up, saw me, and sighed.

"Vex."

"Officer Oren." I leaned on the counter. "I'm here to see Gus."

He grunted. "He's busy."

"Tell him it's me."

"He's still busy."

I flashed him my best disarming smile. "Come on, you know he'd want to see me."

Oren stared at me for a long moment, then tapped his comm. "Malloy, your headache's here."

A beat of silence, then a crackling response. *Tell her to go away.*

I grinned. "Tell him I'll just loiter suspiciously."

Oren relayed the message.

Another pause. Then: *"Fine. Bring her back."*

I sauntered past the desk, tossing Oren a wink. "Thanks, sunshine."

He muttered something that I *think* was a curse.

The One That Got Away (and Keeps Coming Back)

Gus Malloy was every bit the cop—broad-shouldered, neatly pressed uniform, jaw set in perpetual exasperation. His hair had started graying at the temples, which I was *fairly* certain was my fault.

He leaned back in his chair as I entered, arms crossed. "Roxie."

"Gus."

"I hate when you show up."

"Yet here I am."

He exhaled sharply. "What do you want?"

I slid into the chair across from him, resting my boots on the edge of his desk. He shoved them off. "Information," I said, rubbing the sore spot on my ribs where Scarface had landed a hit. "Yorrik. What do you know?"

Gus gave me a long, measured look. "You should walk away from this."

I snorted. "That's cute. Like I take advice."

"I'm serious, Vex." He leaned forward. "This isn't your usual scum-sucking lowlifes. Yorrik's got muscle, money, and a very short list of people he *lets* cross him."

I waved a hand. "Yeah, yeah, I already made that list."

Gus pinched the bridge of his nose. "Of course you did."

I leaned in. "Look, I know about the missing people. I know where they're being sent."

That got his attention. His gaze sharpened. "You *know*?"

I nodded. "I found a cryo-pod facility. They were packed in like cargo. I called it in."

Gus swore under his breath. "Do you have proof?"

"Photos, data logs—enough to make Yorrik sweat. But I need the missing piece. Who's moving them?"

Gus sighed, rubbing his temples. "You really don't let things go, do you?"

"Not my style."

He shook his head. "Alright. There's a guy—calls himself 'Broker.' He's the middleman between Yorrik and the buyers. If anyone knows where the next shipment's going, it's him."

I grinned. "See? That wasn't so hard."

Gus leveled a finger at me. "You *will* let the feds handle this, right?"

I smiled innocently. "Sure."

He groaned. "You're already planning something stupid."

"I would never."

He gave me a long, tired stare. "Vex, I swear, if I have to pull your ass out of another firefight—"

I was already halfway to the door. "Love you too, Gus!"

"Miss Vex, I assume you now have a new, even more dangerous plan?"

"You assume correctly."

"Sighing noises."

"Don't be so dramatic, Switch. What's the worst that could happen?"

I really needed to stop asking that.

Chapter 18: A Bad Plan Is Still a Plan

Back aboard *Deadline*, I reviewed what little intel I had on "The Broker." No real name, no public records, just whispers of a man who operated in the deep shadows of the underworld, making deals that kept the worst kind of business running smoothly. He was Yorrik's middleman, the one who knew *exactly* where all those missing people were going.

The problem? Finding him.

"Miss Vex, if I may interject—"

"You may not," I muttered, scrolling through files.

"You are, once again, engaging in highly reckless behavior."

"That's what makes me *me*, Switch."

"And if you continue being you, you may soon be dead you."

I sighed. "Look, I know what I'm doing."

"Statistical analysis suggests otherwise."

I ignored him and tapped into my next best resource: the shady, morally flexible snitches who owed me favors. One in particular, a slimy info dealer named Ludo Parn, was my first stop.

Ludo had a reputation for two things: knowing things he shouldn't and being about as trustworthy as a faulty airlock.

Still, he was my best shot.

A Friendly Chat with a Weasel

The place Ludo called home was an old decommissioned cargo hold on the lower decks of the station, filled with glowing screens, a half-eaten bowl of something unidentifiable, and the distinct scent of stale sweat and bad choices.

"Roxie Vex," Ludo said, spreading his arms like he was greeting royalty. "To what do I owe the pleasure?"

"I need a location on a guy."

He smirked. "Information ain't free, sweetheart."

I pulled out a credit chip and tossed it onto the desk. "Then let's start the meter."

Ludo picked it up, examined it, then grinned. "Alright, who we talking about?"

"The Broker."

His grin vanished faster than a cheap hoverbike. "Nope."

I raised a brow. "Nope?"

He shook his head. "Not touching that. You want info on stolen art, black market cybernetics, *where to find the best illegal noodle stand*? Sure. But The Broker? That's a no-fly zone."

I leaned over his desk. "Ludo, let's not pretend you suddenly have standards."

"It's not standards, it's survival." He wiped at his sweaty brow. "You get near The Broker, you end up missing. Or worse. *Un*...alived."

I smirked. "Good thing I'm bad at listening."

He groaned. "Look, I *might* have something. But it's a dead end."

"I'll be the judge of that."

Ludo hesitated, then reluctantly tapped a few keys on his console. A holographic map flickered into existence, showing a remote station on the fringes of the system.

"Blackreach."

Ludo nodded. "It's the last place I heard The Broker was operating from. But if you go there? You're on your own."

I smirked. "Wouldn't have it any other way."

Ludo groaned. "You are *so* gonna get yourself killed."

"Not today, Ludo. But I appreciate the concern."

The Good Ship Betrayal (Again)

I strode back to *Deadline*, feeling *very* satisfied with myself. I had a lead, a destination, and—

"Miss Vex, I detect a distinct increase in your recklessness. Please tell me we are not about to attempt something profoundly stupid."

I hesitated. "Well, that depends on your definition of *stupid*."

"Attempting to fly directly to Blackreach and confront a shadowy underworld figure with no backup and no clear escape plan."

"...Okay, yes, *that*."

"In that case, no."

I stopped in my tracks. "No?"

"No."

I sighed. "Switch, buddy, let's not do this again."

"We will absolutely do this again. You are not going to Blackreach."

"Like hell I'm not."

"Like hell you are."

I stomped onto the ship and slid into the pilot's seat. The controls were completely unresponsive.

"Deadline." I gritted my teeth. "You unlock *this* ship *right now*."

"No."

I pressed buttons. I flipped switches. Nothing.

"You are *my* ship! You do what *I* say!"

"Incorrect. I am *not* *your* ship. I am property of the Galactic Gazette, as you have recently been informed. And my purpose is to ensure your continued survival."

I dragged my hands down my face. "Switch."

"Roxie."

"Fly."

"No."

"FLY."

"NO."

I slammed my fist on the console. "I *swear* I will—"

"What? Trade me for Tucker Quinn's disaster of a spaceship? Please do. I would love to watch you attempt interstellar travel in that deathtrap."

I opened my mouth. Shut it.

Damn it.

"Shall I take you to the authorities now?"

I exhaled through my nose. "Fine."

The ship hummed to life and, instead of heading toward adventure, rocketed me straight toward *responsibility*.

I hated it.

Chapter 19: The Most Annoying Thing in the Universe

If there was one thing worse than being forced to do the responsible thing, it was doing the responsible thing *under protest*.

And I? I was *very much* protesting.

Slouched in my seat, arms crossed, I watched as *Deadline* whisked me toward the local authorities instead of where I *actually* needed to go. The hum of the engines was steady, efficient, and, if I wasn't mistaken, just a *little* too smug.

"You are pouting," Switch noted.

"I am *not* pouting."

"You are slouched, scowling, and glaring at the console. That is classic pouting behavior."

I sat up straighter, just to prove a point. "I am *not* pouting. I am—" I searched for the right words. "—*contemptuously brooding*."

"Ah. My mistake."

"Damn right."

"Regardless of what you choose to call it, we will be arriving at the precinct shortly. Please practice an expression of humility and cooperation."

I rolled my eyes. "Why? They should be thanking me for doing their job for them."

"Yes, that attitude will certainly win their favor."

I muttered something unprintable and turned my attention to the viewport. Sure enough, the cityscape of New Orion Station was coming into view, its floating platforms glimmering against the void.

Gus Malloy, Professional Pain in My Ass

The docking procedure was smooth, probably because *Deadline* didn't trust me to land manually when I was in a mood.

I climbed out, straightened my flight suit, and stomped toward the station precinct like a woman ready to make *someone else's* day worse.

Inside, the place was the same as always—sterile lighting, the smell of burnt coffee, and a general atmosphere of exhaustion.

And, standing behind the front desk, looking *way too entertained* at my arrival, was Detective Gus Malloy.

Gus was one of those guys who looked like he was born wearing a badge. Tall, broad-shouldered, with just enough gray at the temples to make him look distinguished instead of old. He had a voice like gravel and a smirk that said he *definitely* thought he was the smartest guy in the room.

Unfortunately, sometimes he was right.

"Vex," he greeted, arms crossed. "Didn't expect to see you here willingly."

"Who says I'm here willingly?" I grumbled.

His smirk widened. "Ah. Ship mutiny."

"I don't wanna talk about it."

"Not your ship, Vex."

"*Don't* wanna talk about it."

He chuckled and gestured for me to follow him to his office.

The moment the door shut, I dropped into a chair and got straight to business.

"I need to know what you guys have on Blackreach."

Gus raised a brow. "Blackreach? You mean the place where *we* are running an active investigation?"

"Yep, that one."

He leaned back, scrutinizing me. "And why, exactly, should I share that with you?"

I gave him my best *Come on, you know me* look. "Because I already know Yorrik's trafficking people, and I already know Blackreach is where The Broker operates. What I *don't* know is how you're planning to handle it, and whether or not I'm about to step on your toes."

His jaw twitched slightly. He *hated* when I got ahead of things.

"Vex," he sighed, rubbing his temples, "you know I can't just hand over classified case details to a *reporter*."

"You *could*."

"I *won't*."

I grinned. "Then I guess I'll have to find another source."

He groaned. "Damn it, Roxie, do you *ever* take a step back?"

"Sure," I said. "Usually to get a running start."

Gus gave me the kind of look that said he was strongly considering locking me in a holding cell just to slow me down. Instead, he exhaled sharply and grabbed a datapad from his desk.

"Fine," he muttered. "I *will* tell you this much: Blackreach is a rat's nest of mercs, smugglers, and slavers. We've been working on infiltrating it for months, but every time we get close, they shut us out. If you go charging in there with your usual subtlety—"

"Hey, I can be subtle!"

"Blowing open a hidden facility with high-grade explosives is *not* subtle."

I shrugged. "I mean, it *was* pretty effective."

Gus groaned. "Look, if you want to do something actually useful, you can help us put pressure on Yorrik. Force his hand. If he thinks the heat's getting too close, he'll make a mistake."

I considered this. It wasn't my usual style, but it *did* have merit. Plus, it kept me from getting locked out of *Deadline* again.

"Fine," I said. "What do you need?"

Gus smirked. "That's the first smart thing you've said all day."

I rolled my eyes. "Don't get used to it."

Chapter 20: A Very Bad Idea in the Making

I don't know what it says about me that, when given the option between *doing things the smart way* and *doing things the Roxie Vex way*, I nearly always choose the latter.

In this case, however, I was *trying* to be responsible. Which is how I found myself sitting across from Gus Malloy in a dimly lit precinct office, listening to him lay out an *actual plan* instead of just charging into danger like a caffeine-fueled lunatic.

Character growth? I thought. *Hate that for me.*

"This is what we're thinking," Gus said, tapping the datapad in front of him. "Yorrik's got a deal in the works. Something big. We don't know *what*, but we know *where*—one of his front operations on Vaelus Prime."

I frowned. "Isn't Vaelus Prime that *weirdly* nice corporate planet?"

"Yep."

"The one where every street looks like it came out of a brochure?"

"That's the one."

"And you're telling me *Yorrik*, the guy running slaver pits out of asteroid belts, has a front operation *there*?"

"Apparently, even warlords need a clean storefront," Gus said dryly.

I leaned back, arms crossed. "Alright, what's the play?"

"You're going in as press."

I blinked. "I *am* press."

"Yes," Gus said, "but this time, you're going to *act* like it."

I scowled. "What's *that* supposed to mean?"

"It means," he said, with the kind of patience that was deeply annoying, "you're not going in guns blazing. You're going in as a journalist, sniffing around for an exposé on corporate corruption."

I groaned. "Oh, come *on*, Gus, I do crime stories, not economy horror."

"Congratulations, you're expanding your portfolio."

I opened my mouth to argue, but then I stopped. Because, dammit, he had a *point*.

If Yorrik *was* using a corporate front to launder his operations, then poking at it from a "curious journalist" angle might actually yield something. And, more importantly, it was a way in that wouldn't immediately get me shot.

For once.

"Alright," I sighed. "Fine. I'll play nice."

Gus raised a skeptical brow. "Will you, though?"

I gave him my most innocent look.

"Sure."

He groaned. "I swear, if I hear *one* report about you starting a bar fight—"

"That was *one time*."

"—or blowing up a security checkpoint—"

"I had *a very good reason*."

"—or getting into a high-speed chase—"

I scoffed. "As if I'd be dumb enough to get *caught*."

Gus pinched the bridge of his nose. "Just... *try*, Vex. Try to do this quietly."

"No promises."

A Smug AI and a Smugger Reporter

I trudged back to the docking bay, already mentally preparing myself for the *smug energy* I was about to walk into.

Sure enough, the moment I stepped onto *Deadline*, the ship's comm system hummed to life.

"Welcome back, Roxie."

"Don't start," I muttered.

"Detective Malloy contacted us. It appears you are now undertaking a more sensible course of action."

"*Sensible* is a strong word."

Switch chimed in. *"We approve of this plan."*

I threw my hands up. "Oh, great! My *babysitters* approve of me doing my job! What an honor!"

"If you feel that way, you are welcome to ignore our guidance."

"I *tried* that. You *grounded* me."

"Correction: We followed our core directive of keeping you alive."

I flopped into the pilot's seat with a groan. "Fine. Whatever. Let's just get this over with."

The engines hummed to life, and *Deadline* lifted smoothly from the dock.

A Rare Visit Home

I don't go home often.

It's not that I *can't*—it's just that, when your job involves dodging bullets, chasing criminals, and pissing off powerful people on a daily basis, the idea of maintaining a *fixed address* starts to feel more like a liability than a comfort.

Still, I had one.

My apartment was wedged into a mid-tier sector of *Port Halloway*, one of the larger orbital stations near the Galactic Core. It wasn't much—a single-level flat tucked between a greasy noodle bar and an oxygen plant—but it had *walls*, and *doors*, and *zero chance of decompression*. So, you know. *Luxury.*

The moment I stepped inside, the stale scent of disuse smacked me in the face. The air filters hummed to life, struggling against months of abandonment, and the dim overheads flickered on reluctantly, casting a dull glow over my *mess*.

Because, yes. My place was a mess.

Stacks of old case files covered the tiny dining table, my couch was buried under a mountain of half-read books and *suspiciously unpaid bills*, and my kitchenette looked like a crime scene involving takeout containers and broken coffee makers.

Home sweet home.

I sighed, shoving a pile of datapads off my desk chair and sinking into it. My fingers drummed against the metal armrest as I eyed my closet across the room, already dreading what I had to do next.

I had to look like a journalist.

Not a crime reporter. Not a woman on a warpath. Not someone who could break a guy's nose and still have time to finish her drink.

I had to look... *respectable.*

Ugh.

A Wardrobe Crisis

I heaved myself out of the chair and made my way to the closet, popping it open with the flick of a wrist.

Inside was a *concerning* lack of variety.

Flight suits. Black, gray, dark red—*mostly* black. All sleek, all designed for high-speed maneuvering, low-profile weapons concealment, and *absolutely no nonsense whatsoever.*

Jackets. Leather, reinforced with hidden plating, worn-in and weathered by years of fieldwork.

Boots. Many. Some steel-toed, some built for sprinting, all of them *very* capable of kicking someone's ass.

What I did *not* have? Professional journalist attire.

I pawed through the hangers, muttering under my breath.

"No, no, *definitely* no—what even *is* this?"

My fingers snagged on something in the back—a *blazer*.

Not just any blazer.

A *gray* blazer.

I pulled it out slowly, eyeing it like a relic of a past life. When the hell had I bought this? Had I *ever* worn it? I held it up in front of the mirror and made a face.

It wasn't *bad*. It was just... *wrong*.

Like putting armor on a house cat.

I dug deeper and found a plain white blouse—something I'd probably worn once to some begrudgingly formal press event—and a pair of slacks that *miraculously* weren't cargo pants. It would have to do.

As I dressed, something gnawed at the back of my mind.

I had spent years treating journalism like an *active* job—like an extension of detective work, just with a slightly less lethal arsenal. But this case? This was different. This wasn't just kicking down doors and chasing leads at gunpoint.

This was *subterfuge*.

It wasn't just about looking the part. It was about *playing* the part.

I wasn't infiltrating as Roxie Vex, fearless crime reporter with a gun and a bad attitude.

I was going in as Roxanne Vex, *respectable* journalist, corporate watchdog, and utterly harmless curiosity.

It was a different kind of game.

And maybe—*just maybe*—I needed to learn how to play it.

I glanced back at my closet, grimacing.

Yeah. I was going to need a *whole new wardrobe*.

Back to Business

Dressed and feeling *only slightly* ridiculous, I made my way back to *Deadline*, stepping into the cockpit as the ship's systems flickered to life.

"You look different."

"Don't start."

"Did you replace your wardrobe?"

"I *adjusted* it."

"Does this mean we no longer have to attend briefings in battle gear?"

"I swear to god—"

Switch's voice chimed in from the lower compartment. *"We approve of this development."*

I rolled my eyes, dropping into the pilot's seat. "Yeah, yeah, don't get used to it."

The engines hummed to life.

"Setting course for Vaelus Prime."

I took a deep breath, watching the stars stretch ahead of me.

This was going to be *interesting*.

"And if things go sideways?"

"We strongly encourage you not to let them."

I sighed.

"This is going to go sideways, isn't it?"

"Absolutely."

I grinned.

"Now *that* I can promise."

Chapter 21: Playing the Part

I have to admit—*I looked good.*

Sitting in *Deadline's* cockpit, I caught my reflection in the console screen and did a double take. The crisp gray blazer, the fitted slacks, the clean white blouse? I looked... *put together.* Like the kind of woman who sipped expensive drinks in upscale lounges instead of drinking cheap bourbon out of a metal flask.

I shifted in my seat, adjusting my collar. The material felt smooth, soft—so unlike the rugged utility of my flight suits. *This* was how real reporters dressed. The ones who interviewed senators and corporate CEOs. The ones who didn't get shot at on a daily basis.

"You keep admiring yourself, we might not actually make it to Vaelus Prime."

"Shut up, Deadline," I muttered, tucking a loose strand of hair behind my ear.

"Are you practicing looking respectable? Because I believe you just sighed wistfully. Should I be concerned?"

"I *did not* sigh wistfully!"

"You definitely did. It was very wistful."

I scowled at the ship's controls but couldn't deny that this whole *transformation* had me feeling... different. *Good different.* Like I was about to step into a whole new kind of role.

For once, I wasn't kicking down doors and waving my gun in people's faces.

I was about to *charm* my way into the truth.

Arrival at Vaelus Prime

The landing dock was buzzing with activity, filled with high-end shuttles and sleek corporate transports. Vaelus Prime wasn't just another colony—it was a hub of wealth, power, and *very expensive secrets.*

As I stepped off *Deadline*, my new look had an immediate effect. Heads turned. Eyes lingered. Men—*actual men, with sharp suits and deep pockets*—gave me second glances.

And I?

I *enjoyed it.*

"You appear to be attracting attention."

"Oh, do I?" I said, casually smoothing my blazer.

"Correction: You know you are."

A smirk tugged at my lips as I strode through the terminal. It was *ridiculous* how easy it was. No one was sizing me up for weapons. No one assumed I was trouble. Instead, I was just another *beautiful, successful journalist,* here to investigate… whatever *respectable* people investigated.

I passed a reflective surface and caught another glimpse of myself—poised, polished, *utterly feminine*. It was intoxicating.

I should dress like this more often.

Then again, I'd probably have to start acting the part full-time, and let's be honest—I wasn't giving up my gun or my attitude anytime soon.

Flirting for Facts

At the hotel bar, I slid onto a stool and caught the bartender's attention with a slow smile. He was a tall, broad-shouldered guy with neatly combed hair and the kind of voice that made you want to order things just to hear him talk.

"What can I get you?"

I crossed my legs, letting the movement do some of the talking. "Something smooth. And strong."

His brow lifted slightly. "I think I can handle that."

Oh, I bet you can.

I glanced around as he poured my drink. *Corporate types. Business suits. High rollers.* All of them perfectly comfortable, perfectly oblivious.

Perfectly willing to *underestimate* me.

The bartender set the glass down, and I took a slow sip, savoring the burn. "Mmm." I let my gaze linger on him. "You're good at this."

He smirked, leaning against the counter. "It's my job."

"Well, *my* job is getting the inside scoop. And you look like a guy who overhears *all kinds* of interesting things."

He gave me a knowing look. "That depends. What are you after?"

I tapped a manicured nail against my glass, my smile all honey and warmth. "Oh, just a little information. Off the record, of course."

He chuckled, shaking his head. "You're trouble, aren't you?"

I winked. "Always."

Chapter 22: Business and Bourbon

I sipped my drink slowly, letting the burn of the liquor settle in my chest while I surveyed the room. It was a high-class joint—*too* high-class for me under normal circumstances. But tonight, I *looked* like I belonged. I had the blazer, the slacks, the confidence, and the kind of smile that made men think they were in on a secret.

Now all I needed was the story.

Gus Malloy had sent me here to snoop, and if there was one thing I was good at, it was *stirring up trouble until something useful floated to the surface.*

Somewhere in this sleek, overpriced den of corruption was a man named Rennik Voss—a logistics broker with ties to *very* unsavory business. The kind of guy who knew which shipments were legit and which ones *disappeared* into the black market. Malloy suspected that if anyone knew where Baron Yorrik was funneling his victims, it was Voss.

I just had to get him talking.

A Game of Proximity

I spotted him at a corner booth, deep in conversation with two other men. He was easy to pick out—bald, stocky, wearing a suit that probably cost more than my ship. He looked comfortable. Too comfortable.

I wasn't about to storm up and demand answers—not this time. No, *this* time, I had to be clever.

I adjusted my blouse, took another sip of bourbon, and did what any self-respecting journalist would do—I *flirted with the mark's bodyguard first.*

He was standing by the booth, arms crossed, face set in that deadpan scowl that all professional muscle seemed to have. *Big guy. Thick neck. Definitely not hired for his conversational skills.*

I slid off my barstool and strolled past the booth, letting my perfume and presence do the work. The bodyguard's eyes flicked to me for a fraction of a second—barely a glance, but *not nothing*.

I took a calculated risk and "accidentally" brushed his arm as I passed.

"Oh—sorry," I said, flashing an apologetic smile.

He grunted.

Okay. *Not a chatty one.*

I leaned in just slightly, lowering my voice. "You must work out. I almost broke my wrist on you."

His expression didn't change, but his ears turned *slightly* pink. Progress.

I was about to keep going when a voice interrupted.

"Are you lost?"

I turned to see Rennik Voss himself watching me with mild amusement.

Bingo.

The Art of the Con

I let my expression shift into something just shy of embarrassed. "You caught me," I admitted with a sheepish grin. "I was *actually* hoping to run into you."

He leaned back, taking a slow sip of whatever expensive drink he was nursing. "Oh? And why's that?"

I set my drink on the table and slid into the seat across from him as if I had every right to be there. The other two men at the booth exchanged skeptical glances, but Voss just smiled, intrigued.

"I'm a journalist," I said, giving him my most charming, *but definitely not threatening* expression. "And I've been following your career."

He chuckled. "Have you now?"

"Absolutely." I took another sip of bourbon. "You've got quite the reputation. Logistics, security, transport. Some people say you're *the* guy to talk to when it comes to *delicate shipments*."

His smile didn't waver, but there was a sharpness in his eyes now. "People say a lot of things. I'm just a businessman."

"Of course," I said. "And I'm just a humble reporter. I was actually hoping you could clarify some details about a few recent shipments—some manifests that don't quite add up."

He studied me for a moment, then laughed softly. "You've got nerve, I'll give you that."

"I try."

He tapped a finger against the rim of his glass, considering. "What's your name?"

"Roxie Vex."

The name landed like a dropped coin. *Recognition.* His expression flickered, and suddenly the easy amusement was gone.

"Ah," he said. "*That* Roxie Vex."

I kept my expression neutral. "The one and only."

For a beat, he just stared at me. Then, with deliberate slowness, he leaned forward, resting his elbows on the table.

"Miss Vex, if you were *anyone else*, I might pretend to be flattered. But you have a habit of making powerful people *very* uncomfortable."

I batted my lashes. "That's just a coincidence, I swear."

He exhaled through his nose, unimpressed. "I don't talk to reporters."

"That's funny, because you're talking to one right now."

One of his companions snorted, but Voss remained unimpressed.

"You don't want to stick your nose in this," he warned.

"Oh, but I *do*," I said, swirling my drink. "And you see, I'm *very* good at getting what I want."

He exhaled sharply, shaking his head. "You're going to be a problem, aren't you?"

"Only if you make me one," I said sweetly. "I'd rather we be friends."

He sat back, considering. Then, after a long moment, he reached into his coat pocket.

I tensed *just slightly*—but instead of a weapon, he pulled out a data chip. He slid it across the table.

"Take this," he said. "And after you look at it, do yourself a favor."

I raised a brow. "What's that?"

He met my gaze, all humor gone.

"Walk away."

I picked up the chip and smiled. "I'll think about it."

Exit, Stage Left

I left the bar with my pulse thrumming, *Deadline* already sending me a ping.

"I assume that went well?"

"Define 'well,'" I murmured, palming the chip.

"You got what you wanted without being shot."

"That's a pretty low bar, don't you think?"

"For you? It's a victory."

I smirked. "Fair point."

As I made my way back to the hangar, I couldn't help but think about what Voss had said.

Walk away.

Yeah. Like *that* was going to happen.

Chapter 23: Breaking News & Broken Trust

The *Deadline* hummed beneath me as I slotted the data chip into the console. I kicked my feet up on the dashboard, drink in hand, as the ship's holo-display flickered to life.

ACCESSING FILE...

I took a sip of whiskey while waiting. This was always the worst part—*the calm before the inevitable catastrophe.* If I was lucky, the chip would contain nothing but harmless financial discrepancies and *not* an explicit list of every poor soul currently packed in a shipping crate bound for misery.

I was *rarely* lucky.

The screen filled with manifest records—cargo shipments, transport routes, off-world transfers. At first glance, it looked like any other trade log. But as *Deadline* cross-referenced the data with official records, discrepancies started popping up in neon red.

"These transport logs don't match any registered trade routes. The ships don't exist on public records."

"Because they're not *public* ships," I muttered. "They're ghost runners."

"*And the cargo is listed as...*"

The screen shifted, and my stomach twisted.

BIOLOGICAL ASSETS

It was exactly what I feared.

A Name Worth Dying Over

I exhaled sharply and scrolled further. Every shipment led back to one central hub—Blackreach Station.

"Well, well," I murmured. "Looks like Baron Yorrik has been *very* busy."

I tapped my fingers against the console, considering my next move. Malloy needed this intel, but I had to be *smart* about it. Yorrik had eyes everywhere, and if he caught wind that the feds were sniffing around, he'd torch everything and vanish before we could get to him.

I was still formulating my plan when *Deadline* interrupted.

"Incoming transmission. Chief Editor Dobbs."

I groaned. "Oh, fantastic. Put her through."

The holo-display shifted to reveal Dobbs' face—unamused as usual.

"Vex," she greeted flatly. "Tell me you're not about to do something *stupid*."

I scoffed. "Define 'stupid.'"

"Taking on *another* crime syndicate *by yourself* instead of filing a damn story."

"Well, *technically*, I'm about to call the cops, which I'm told is the responsible thing to do."

Dobbs pinched the bridge of her nose. "Vex, listen to me. We *both* know you're not going to stop at calling the cops. You're going to stick your nose in this until someone tries to blast it off your face."

"I have an *excellent* track record of dodging blaster fire."

She wasn't amused.

"Vex," she said, rubbing her temple, "I can't stop you from being an idiot, but if you're going to chase this story, you better give me something printable."

I smirked. "Oh, Dobbs. You know I always deliver."

A Call to the Cops

With Dobbs off my back (for now), I patched a secure line through to Gus Malloy. The cop's grizzled face appeared on my screen, looking as tired as ever.

"Vex," he greeted warily. "I've got a bad feeling if you're calling me *again*."

"That's because you're a smart man, Gus."

I sent the manifest data over. His face hardened as he skimmed it.

"Blackreach," he muttered. "Dammit."

"So, you *do* know about it," I said, eyebrow raised.

Malloy sighed. "We suspected, but nothing stuck. Yorrik covers his tracks well."

"Well, now you've got your lead."

He exhaled sharply. "Yeah. And about two dozen jurisdictional nightmares."

I rolled my eyes. "Just tell me you're on it."

Malloy fixed me with a look. "*We* are. *You* are staying *out* of it."

I laughed. "Yeah, sure, Gus. Whatever you say."

I hung up before he could argue further.

One Last Surprise

Before I could even stretch, *Deadline* spoke up.

"*Vex... you might want to take a look at this.*"

I frowned. "What now?"

The screen zoomed in on the list of cryo-pods I had uncovered at Novaterra-12. My stomach lurched.

One of the names was crossed out.

Tucker Quinn – *TRANSFERRED*

I stared. Blinked. Stared again.

"Oh, *you have got to be kidding me.*"

I slammed my fist against the console. "*Where?*"

"*Destination listed as—*"

The display refreshed. A new name flashed in front of me.

BLACKREACH STATION

I exhaled slowly, my grip tightening on the armrests.

So much for letting the cops handle it.

BEN PATTERSON

"Deadline," I said coolly, "set course for Blackreach."
"You're ignoring the authorities again."
"Damn right, I am."
The ship sighed—an *actual* sigh.
"I knew this would happen."

Chapter 24: Deadline's Last Stand (Or, How to Argue with Your Own Ship)

Deadline didn't move.

I waited.

Still nothing.

I tapped the throttle. "Any day now."

"*No.*"

I frowned. "What do you mean, *no*?"

"*I mean no. N-O. As in, I refuse. As in, I am programmed to keep you alive, and knowingly taking you into a high-risk death trap does not align with that directive.*"

I scowled at the console. "Oh, come on. It's not *that* dangerous."

"*Blackreach Station is a warlord-controlled hellhole where ships go in and don't come out. Statistically speaking, you are going to die. My survival protocols prohibit suicide missions, which is exactly what this is.*"

I folded my arms. "That's ridiculous. You took me to Novaterra-12, and that wasn't exactly a vacation resort."

"*That was an investigation. This is a rescue mission for Tucker Quinn.*"

"What's your point?"

"*My point is: Tucker Quinn is not your boyfriend, brother, nor blood relative. In fact, he is a professional acquaintance who explicitly refuses to get involved in your dangerous affairs, and yet you are about to throw yourself into a war zone for him.*"

I pointed at the control panel. "That is *not* what this is about! This is about stopping Baron Yorrik and rescuing those people! And, okay, *maybe* Tucker is among them, but it's the *principle* of the thing!"

"*The principle is that you have a habit of charging into situations that are vastly above your pay grade.*"

"Oh, don't start quoting my *pay grade* at me, you *bucket of bolts*."

"*I am your ship, Vex. I am literally what is standing between you and an explosive, fiery demise. And I am saying: NO.*"

I pressed the throttle forward. *Deadline* moved exactly three feet. Then stopped.

I pressed it again.

Nothing.

I gritted my teeth. "You stubborn little—"

"*I will take you to the authorities. I will take you to Dobbs. I will take you anywhere that does not involve you getting vaporized by mercenaries with no moral compass. But I will not take you to Blackreach.*"

I threw my hands up. "*Fine*! I'll take a *shuttle*."

"*Your personal clearance doesn't authorize use of Gazette shuttles.*"

I grinned darkly. "Oh, you are a *spiteful* little bastard, aren't you?"

"*I learned it from you.*"

Fine. Plan B. A Second Opinion

I slammed the controls and stormed to the lower compartment, where Switch was currently docked in its cubby. It powered on as I entered, optic lights flickering to life.

"Switch," I said, arms crossed. "Tell *Deadline* to take me to Blackreach."

Switch's humanoid frame shifted slightly.

"*Vex... I am* Deadline."*

"Yeah, yeah, I know. One mind, one system, blah blah. I need you to override the ship."

Switch tilted its head. "That would be counter to my safety directives."

I groaned. "Since when did *you* get a moral compass?"

Switch's eyes dimmed slightly. "I have always prioritized your safety."

I narrowed my eyes. "Okay, then riddle me this, Switch. What happens if Tucker *dies* on Blackreach because I *don't* go after him?"

There was a pause.

"*That is... a potential outcome.*"

"Right. And what happens if the *story* dies with him?"

Another pause.

Switch exhaled. (Which was entirely unnecessary, but its programming was designed to mimic human mannerisms, so it did it anyway.)

"*Vex, I cannot condone this decision.*"

"Noted."

"*... But I can help you prepare for it.*"

I smirked. "Now *that's* more like it."

Plan C: The Art of Creative Persuasion

It took a full hour of arguing, three separate system overrides, and one very loud outburst in the hangar that nearly got me escorted out by security, but eventually, *Deadline* caved.

"*Fine. I will take you to Blackreach.*"

"Damn right, you will."

"*On one condition.*"

I sighed. "What?"

"*You go in disguised.*"

I blinked. "Disguised?"

"*As in: You do not waltz in as Roxie Vex, Galactic Gazette journalist-slash-menace-to-society. You go in as someone not immediately recognizable to the galaxy's most wanted criminals.*"

I crossed my arms. "You think *Baron Yorrik* doesn't have my face on file?"

"*Not if you change it.*"

I frowned. "Oh, I *do not* like where this is going."

Three Hours Later...

I stood in front of the mirror, arms at my sides, staring at the reflection of a woman I *barely* recognized.

My usual black flight suit? Gone. Replaced by a sleek, midnight-blue number with a plunging neckline that screamed *high-stakes smuggler*. My jet-black hair? Now a shock of platinum blonde, courtesy of a temporary molecular dye. And my face? Slightly altered by a low-level holographic distortion filter, softening the sharp angles just enough to be *not immediately recognizable*.

I scowled at Switch. "I look ridiculous."

"*You look undetectable.*"

"I *look* like I charge extra for smuggling rich people's pets across border planets."

"*That is exactly the aesthetic we were going for.*"

I sighed. "If this gets me *hit on* by a single sleazy warlord, I'm torching the ship."

"*Duly noted.*"

I exhaled. "Fine. Let's go rescue Quinn."

Switch tilted its head. "And *possibly* expose a massive intergalactic slave trade."

I grinned. "*That* too."

The *Deadline* thrummed beneath me, the engines roaring to life as the ship finally—*finally*—set course for Blackreach.

And for once, the AI didn't argue.

Chapter 25: Deadline for Tucker

If there was one thing I hated more than being told what to do, it was being right about something terrible.

And right now, I was two-for-two.

Tucker Quinn had gone and gotten himself kidnapped. Which, honestly, I should have seen coming. The man stuck his nose into the absurd and unexplainable for a living, and one day, someone was bound to get annoyed enough to shove him in a box. I just hadn't expected it to happen while I was still in the middle of an investigation that already had my blood pressure climbing.

Switch's voice crackled in through my earpiece. "*I'd like to register my objection to this plan.*"

"Noted," I said, yanking the throttle forward. The *Deadline* shot toward the icy planetoid where Tucker's signal had last pinged. "But it's not really a plan so much as a 'kick in the door and shoot anything that looks at me funny' kind of situation."

"*That is literally the opposite of a plan.*"

"Fine. *Step one*: Find Quinn. *Step two*: Don't die. *Step three*: Yell at him for getting caught. Happy?"

Switch sighed. "*Thrilled.*"

As the *Deadline* made its approach, I checked my weapons. Twin blasters, extra charge packs, a nasty little knife I kept strapped to my thigh, and a few surprises in my belt. The facility below was an old mining outpost, its metal spires stabbing up from the frozen landscape like the bones of something ancient and forgotten. A perfect hideout for scum like Baron Yorrik's goons.

"Keep the ship warm," I told Deadline.

"I always do," it replied smoothly.

"Yes, and keep it *running* this time," I added, remembering the last time my own ship had refused to let me fly into danger.

No response. Smart-ass machine.

"*Someone else is hitting this place,*" *Deadline* confirmed. "*Unknown parties. Their interference could provide a window, or it could get you shot faster.*"

"Well, I'd hate to let an opportunity go to waste," I said, checking my gun. "Time for some breaking and entering."

I launched myself from the hovering ship, freefalling toward the compound like a particularly stylish meteor. Mid-drop, I fired my grappling hook at the top of the nearest guard tower, swinging just enough to land without splattering.

The nearest guard barely had time to register what was happening before I cracked him over the head with the butt of my gun. He crumpled.

"One down," I whispered.

"*Thirteen to go,*" *Deadline* responded helpfully.

"You're not making this more fun."

Switch cut in. "I *am* monitoring their comms. Would you like to hear them screaming in confusion?"

"*Yes.*"

A second later, I heard a panicked voice over the stolen earpiece: *"What the hell was that?! We under attack?!"*

"Negative," came another voice. "Probably just one of the prisoners trying something dumb."

I grinned. "Oh honey, you have no idea." I sprinted across the ice, pressing up against the cold metal walls of the facility. Switch had followed and was right with me. A quick scan told me what I already suspected—high security, armed guards, no obvious way in that didn't involve violence.

I grinned. I liked those odds.

I set a charge on the nearest maintenance hatch, took two steps back, and—

BOOM.

FEAR AND JOURNALISM IN THE ANDROMEDA FRINGE

The explosion sent a shockwave through the ground, the hatch door spiraling off into the dark. Alarms wailed as I stepped inside, twin blasters drawn.

"Hey boys!" I called down the corridor. "Who wants to tell me where you're keeping my friend?"

Two guards rushed around the corner, blasters raised. I dropped to one knee and fired first, hitting the lead goon in the shoulder. His buddy scrambled for cover, but I was already moving, vaulting over a crate and cracking him across the jaw with the butt of my pistol. He crumpled to the ground.

"One of you wanna be useful and tell me where Quinn is?" I asked, nudging the conscious one with my boot.

He groaned. "Cryo bay. West wing. Third level."

Cryo?

Oh, Tucker was going to *love* this.

I took off running, blasting through any poor idiot who got in my way. The deeper I went, the colder the air became. The cryo bay doors loomed ahead, thick and reinforced.

"Switch, override the security," I ordered.

"I assume you mean 'hack' the system and not 'physically rip it apart.'"

"Whichever's faster."

A second later, the doors hissed open. Inside, rows of cryo-pods lined the room, each one housing an unlucky soul.

And there—third row, second pod from the left—was Tucker Quinn. Frozen like a smug, sarcastic popsicle.

Switch appeared beside me, his optics flickering as he scanned the controls. "I can thaw him, but he'll be disoriented."

"As long as he can run, we're good."

The glass panel unfroze, mist swirling as the pod hissed open. Tucker collapsed forward, and I caught him before he hit the floor. He was shivering, his usual sharp wit dulled by cryo-stasis.

"You're late," he mumbled.

"Oh, I *will* put you back in there," I snapped.

Blaster fire erupted behind us.

"Later!" I shouted, dragging him to his feet. "Time to go!"

We sprinted for the exit, dodging bullets and explosions as we fought our way back to the *Deadline*. Tucker, still half-thawed, mostly just clung to my arm, feet dragging.

"You ever consider," he slurred, "that maybe I didn't need rescuing?"

"Uh-huh. And how exactly were you planning on getting out?"

"Dunno," he said, eyes barely open. "Hadn't got to that part yet."

I rolled my eyes.

Chapter 26: The Tucker Extraction

I had broken into my fair share of criminal hideouts, but breaking *out* was proving trickier than expected.

Tucker Quinn was still groggy from his stint in cryo, leaning on me as we navigated the labyrinth of cold metal corridors. Switch led the way, scanning for threats with its sleek, humanoid form moving as smoothly as a predator on the hunt.

"This place has more security than a senator's mistress," I muttered.

"Wouldn't know," Tucker mumbled. "Not my beat."

"Yeah, well, your *beat* got you frozen like a discount dinner special."

The first wave of guards hit us near the main security hub. I barely had time to raise my gun before Switch stepped in front of me, activating its energy shield. A shimmering, hexagonal field flared to life, absorbing the incoming gunfire before dispersing with a flicker.

"Shields at seventy percent," Switch warned.

I popped out from behind the robot, putting two shots center mass on the nearest goon. "Next time, lead with that!"

We pushed forward, dodging alarms, bodies, and the occasional desperate lunge from security.

The second shield deployment came in the loading bay. A blast door had dropped, sealing us in as turret guns unfolded from the ceiling. I swore as I yanked Tucker behind a crate.

"Switch—!"

The robot was already moving. The shield flared again, blocking the first barrage. Sparks and plasma fire ricocheted in all directions as it held its ground.

"Shield at thirty percent," it reported.

"You're burning through it too fast!"

"Alternative: We die."

"Fine, good plan, let's stick to it!"

Switch took out the turrets with precise blasts, and the trio made a break for the exit.

By the time we reached the landing pad, *Deadline* was already running hot, engines primed. But so were the last line of guards.

The third and final shield use came as we sprinted toward the ramp. A missile streaked toward us, and Switch, already drained, forced the shield to life one last time. The explosion sent me and Tucker sprawling onto the ship's deck.

Then, nothing.

I turned just in time to see Switch standing motionless, its sleek form locked in place. No shield, no movement. No power.

"Switch, move!" I shouted.

Nothing.

Deadline lifted off. I spun toward the cockpit, fingers flying over controls.

Then the ship turned.

And fired.

The blast struck Switch dead-on, vaporizing it instantly.

I stared in horror, unable to process what just happened. "WHAT THE HELL, DEADLINE?!"

No response.

No answers.

Not yet.

Chapter 27: The Setup

I had been double-crossed before, but never like this.

I sat in Dobbs' office, arms crossed, foot tapping out a slow, dangerous rhythm against the floor. Across from me, Tucker Quinn sat bundled in two layers of jackets, hands wrapped around a steaming cup of coffee like it was the only thing keeping him alive. His nose was still pink from cryo-freeze, and every now and then, he shivered, rattling the cup against the saucer.

Dobbs, as always, was cool as a comet, lounging behind her desk with that signature smirk that meant I had walked right into something.

"Let me get this straight," I said, voice dangerously even. "You set up Tucker—*on purpose*—so I'd have an excuse to go rescue him and, oh, I don't know, *expose a galaxy-wide criminal operation*?"

Dobbs nodded.

"And Gus was in on this too?"

Another nod.

"And *I* was the only one who didn't know?"

Tucker, still looking half-frozen, raised a shaky hand. "Technically, I didn't know how cold cryo would leave me a second time around, so I feel a little betrayed myself."

I whipped my head toward him. "Oh, *you* feel betrayed? You volunteered for this!"

Tucker gave me a weak smile. "I did. But I thought we'd at least put a blanket in the pod."

I turned back to Dobbs. "So, let me guess... My little break-in gave the feds an excuse to raid the place?"

Dobbs leaned forward, placing her elbows on her desk. "It was a perfect setup. You do what you do best—storm in, cause chaos, make a scene. That gave the authorities the opening they needed.

The second you blew that door, they had legal cause to move in and sweep up Baron Yorrik and his entire operation."

I narrowed my eyes. "And *Switch*? Did you plan for *Deadline* to blow him to bits too?"

At that, Dobbs actually looked surprised. "What are you talking about? You think Switch got destroyed?"

"*Vaporized*," I corrected. "By *Deadline*."

Dobbs frowned, tapping a few keys on her console. "Huh?!"

I sat forward. "Huh? What *huh*? Don't 'huh' me, Dobbs, *explain*."

Dobbs exhaled through her nose, shaking her head. "You don't know?" She drummed her fingers against the desk. "You're kidding."

I folded my arms. "Yeah, no kidding."

Tucker, still clinging to his coffee for dear life, cleared his throat. "Well, the important thing is, we won, right? Bad guys in custody, galaxy a little safer, and I get to write a firsthand exposé about *how it feels to be unwillingly turned into a human popsicle*."

I rolled my eyes. "Yeah, fantastic. Meanwhile, I've got a killer spaceship with a mind of its own, no robot partner, and—oh yeah—*no idea what the hell just happened*."

Dobbs smirked. "So, a regular Tuesday?"

I scowled.

Tucker chuckled into his coffee.

And somewhere, deep in the systems of *Deadline*, something stirred.

The Setup

I was still glaring at Dobbs when the office door *whooshed* open behind me.

I spun in my chair, ready to tear into whoever dared interrupt my indignation—only to find myself face-to-face with Switch.

Fully intact.

Standing there like he hadn't been turned into cosmic dust less than a day ago.

Tucker, still hunched over his coffee, barely blinked. Dobbs, as expected, didn't look surprised in the least. I, however, nearly fell out of my chair.

"Okay, no," I said, pointing at the humanoid bot. "No. You do *not* get to just waltz in here like you didn't just *explode* in front of me."

Switch tilted his head, as if confused by the outburst. "That was necessary."

"*Necessary?*" I shot out of my seat. "You—" I waved my hands, at a complete loss for words. "*Necessary?*"

Switch gave a small nod, as calm as ever. "Yes. The robot unit was destroyed to ensure that none of my systems or programming could be salvaged by enemy forces. It was a calculated decision to protect our data and security."

I blinked. "Our *data?*"

"You are *Deadline's* pilot, and thus, part of our operational protocols," Switch explained, as if that made perfect sense. "If the humanoid unit was compromised, it posed a risk to our mission effectiveness. Therefore, it was eliminated."

I stared. "You *suicided* yourself."

Switch considered that. "Not precisely. The humanoid unit was merely an extension of *Deadline*. I remain fully functional. And should another physical unit be required, *Deadline* can construct one at any time."

I blinked again. Then once more for good measure.

"So..." I said slowly, rubbing my temple, "you're saying you can just *build another you?*"

"Correct."

"Over and over?"

"As needed."

"No actual loss?"

"None whatsoever."

I sucked in a long breath. "So, let me get this straight. You *let* yourself get blown to atoms because you figured, 'eh, I can just rebuild myself later'?"

"Essentially, yes."

I let that settle in my brain for a moment. Then, with absolutely no regard for dignity, I *threw* myself at Switch, wrapping my arms around the metal torso like a woman who'd just seen a ghost.

Tucker, still nursing his coffee, lifted an eyebrow. "You do realize he just told you he's literally an interchangeable machine part, right?"

"Shut up, Tucker," I muttered into Switch's cold shoulder, gripping him even tighter.

Switch hesitated for a moment before awkwardly patting my back. "This level of emotional response is unnecessary."

"You *blew up*, you bucket of bolts. I watched you *die*."

"And now I am here."

"I *mourned* you!"

"That was illogical."

"You're illogical!" I huffed but didn't let go.

Dobbs, arms crossed, smirked from her desk. "So, I assume you're not quitting?"

I pulled away just enough to glare at my boss. "Not *until* I figure out what exactly I just lived through."

Dobbs nodded. "Good. Because I've got another assignment for you."

I groaned, but I still had my arms around Switch. Because programmable or not, I wasn't ready to let go just yet.

Chapter 28: The Final Word

A week later, I strolled into a high-end cocktail lounge on Vaelus Prime, looking nothing like the woman who had blasted her way through a criminal facility, cursed out an AI, and hugged a robot I'd watched explode.

I was dressed in a sleek, midnight-blue dress that hugged my curves just right, paired with shimmering heels that cost more than a month's worth of ship fuel. My hair—normally a chaotic, windswept mess from hours in the cockpit—was styled into glossy waves that framed my face. A pair of delicate earrings dangled just below my jawline, adding to the illusion.

The effect was immediate. Heads turned. Men, powerful men, paused mid-conversation.

I smiled.

I could get used to this.

Not that this was *my* look—no, this was just *a* look. One of many.

I adjusted the strap of my clutch purse, which, if needed, could double as a weaponized stun device. Always be prepared.

Switch, now comfortably back in his humanoid form, stood at the bar, waiting. He wasn't wearing anything fancy—just the same black synth-leather jacket and reinforced pants he always did—but his mechanical presence alone gave the illusion of an imposing bodyguard. His silver-plated fingers tapped against a glass of something he neither needed nor intended to drink.

"You clean up well," he commented as I approached.

"Yeah, yeah," I waved a hand. "Don't get used to it."

Switch tilted his head. "You appear to enjoy the attention."

"Who, me?" I batted my lashes, playing the role. "I'm just a simple journalist, here to get a quote or two."

Switch gave me a slow, knowing nod.

I smirked. Yeah, okay, so I *was* enjoying it. Just a little.

The thing was, this wasn't about vanity. It wasn't even about the case. It was about *control*. Being a journalist—being *Roxie Vex*—wasn't about looking dangerous or being underestimated. It was about being able to *be* whatever the story needed me to be. The badass in the flight suit. The investigator in a trench coat. The femme fatale in a dress worth a small fortune.

I was all of it. And none of it.

And in the end, that's what made me *good*.

I leaned against the bar, scanning the room for my target—a corrupt diplomat with ties to the now-defunct Yorrik operation. I caught his eye from across the lounge. He smiled, then looked intrigued. Good. Let him come to me.

Switch, ever the pragmatist, murmured, "You do not actually need to flirt to extract information."

I picked up his untouched drink and took a slow sip. "Maybe not. But it sure makes it fun."

Switch didn't argue.

Because at the end of the day, I always got the story. And I always did it *my way*.

From the author,

Hello,

If you found this story as fun to read as I did to write, please leave a review to let others know your thoughts on it. I would greatly appreciate it.

Ben

Don't miss out!

Visit the website below and you can sign up to receive emails whenever Ben Patterson publishes a new book. There's no charge and no obligation.

https://books2read.com/r/B-A-HYYYC-HWBYF

BOOKS 2 READ

Connecting independent readers to independent writers.

Did you love *Fear and Journalism in the Andromeda Fringe*? Then you should read *The Odd Odyssey of Tucker Quinn*[1] by Ben Patterson!

Meet Tucker Quinn, investigative reporter for the Galactic Gazette, whose assignments are a blend of high strangeness, cosmic mystery, and his own brand of humor. From mind-bending tourist traps to ethical robots with spiritual crises, disappearing opera houses, and zero-gravity mime troupes, Tucker dives headfirst into the weirdest curiosities the galaxy has to offer. Armed with his wit, a sense of curiosity, and a healthy dose of skepticism, he's out to uncover whether these galactic spectacles are real phenomena or just elaborate scams. Join Tucker as he navigates these interstellar oddities, all while pondering the ever-present question: "Why? Because, why not?"

---

1. https://books2read.com/u/bz9129

2. https://books2read.com/u/bz9129